PRAISE FOR
THE *NEW YORK TIMES* BESTSELLING
SECOND CHANCE CAT MYSTERIES

"An affirmation of friendship as well as a tantalizing whodunit, *The Whole Cat and Caboodle* marks a promising start to a series sure to appeal to anyone who loves a combination of felonies and felines."

—*Richmond Times-Dispatch*

"Ryan kicks off the new Second Chance Cat Mystery series with a lot of excitement. Her small Maine town is filled with unique characters. . . . This tale is enjoyable from beginning to end; readers will look forward to more." —RT Book Reviews

"If you enjoy a cozy mystery featuring a lovable protagonist with a bevy of staunch friends, a shop you'd love to explore, plenty of suspects, and a supersmart cat, you'll love *The Whole Cat and Caboodle*." —MyShelf.com

"I am absolutely crazy about this series. . . . The cast of characters is phenomenal. . . . I loved every minute of this book." —Melissa's Mochas, Mysteries & Meows

"If you enjoy a lighthearted mystery; a smart, cute cat; and [a] wonderful heroine, then I suggest you read this series."
—The Reading Cafe

"If you are looking for a charming cozy mystery with a smart main character and an adorable cat, then you should check out *The Fast and the Furriest*." —The Avid Reader

FuR LoVe oR MoNeY

A SECOND CHANCE CAT MYSTERY

Sofie Ryan

BERKLEY PRIME CRIME
New York

Fur Love or Money

Chapter 1

"I think it's impossible to take a bad photo of Elvis," Rose said.

"I think you're right," I said.

We were standing in my office more than halfway through the proofs from a photo shoot Elvis had taken part in the day before and there wasn't one image so far that had caught him with his eyes closed or mid-sneeze, which was usually what happened when I had my picture taken. That might have been because Elvis was naturally photogenic, or it might have been because he was a friendly black cat who loved attention.

Elvis had been in a cat show almost a year ago and had attracted the notice of a well-known pet food company. He'd spent most of Monday morning at a photo shoot that was part of a public service campaign funded by the pet food company to encourage people to adopt an older shelter cat. Rose

she said to him. I had a sneaking suspicion a lot of the time he did.

He leaned in for a closer look and then murped his agreement. It seemed he did think Rose was right after all.

Elvis had been a street cat of sorts before he'd ended up with me. It made him the perfect choice for a campaign urging people to think about adopting an older pet. I had no idea how he had ended up here in North Harbor, but the scar that cut diagonally across his nose and the others that were covered by his fur suggested he had been on his own for a while. On the other hand, Elvis was friendly and sociable and had had no problem adjusting to living with me. I had never thought of myself as a "cat person" but now I couldn't imagine life without him.

"I don't have any input into which photos they'll end up using," I said to Rose. "They just sent these to me as a courtesy. I'm not even sure who's going to make the final decision."

She waved away my words with one hand. "It doesn't matter, dear," she said. "They're all wonderful." She smiled at Elvis. "You're doing a very good thing, helping other cats find homes." Then she leaned over and kissed my cheek. "You did a good thing, too."

I frowned at her. "What do you mean?"

"You donated Elvis's fee to our no-kill shelter."

"How did you know that?" I said. I should have guessed Rose would find out. I had never been able to keep anything a secret from her.

Rose and Elvis weren't the only ones who had work to do.

I went downstairs to find Rose and Elvis showing two women the sideboard I had finished painting less than a week ago. It was close to four feet long with sliding glass doors. I had painted it a pale shade of green called glacier. It had taken a lot of sanding and scraping to restore the piece, which, when I bought it, had been painted a muddy shade of brown with two pieces of garish orange-flowered wallpaper glued to the top.

Second Chance was a repurpose store, a place where discarded furniture and other items got a second chance instead of ending up in a landfill or a corner of someone's basement. It was also pretty much the focus of my life at the moment. The shop was in a two-story, redbrick building from the late 1800s in North Harbor, Maine. We were a short walk from the harbor front, and easy to get to from the highway—which meant we saw a lot of tourists. We sold everything from furniture to housewares to refurbished linens. Our stock came from a lot of different places: yard sales, flea markets, people looking to declutter or downsize. I bought regularly from several trash pickers. Rose worked for me part-time when she wasn't busy being the senior version of Nancy Drew.

I caught her eye and pointed toward the back door. She gave an almost imperceptible nod. I cut through the workroom, went out the back door and started across the parking lot toward the old garage that had been turned into more working space and

jest, but that bottle of vodka is the key to getting rid of all those stickers."

"Oh, do tell," I said, folding my arms across my chest and eyeing him with more than a little skepticism.

"All I need to do is soak a cloth with the vodka, lay it on a sticker and then a few minutes later come back and scrape it off."

I studied the three lockers. There were a lot of stickers covering the outside—band stickers, shoe stickers, stickers with positive affirmations and some with four-letter words—and almost as many inside. Even if the vodka trick worked, Mac still had a lot of scraping ahead.

"It'll work," he said. He could probably see the doubt on my face. "I have it on good authority."

I looked over my shoulder at him. "And who exactly is this good authority?"

"Alfred."

"Mr. P.?" I said. Mr. P., aka Alfred Peterson, was a licensed private investigator, a computer whiz and Rose's gentleman friend. She balked at the use of the word "boyfriend."

Mac nodded. "Yes. C'mon, you've said he's one of the smartest people you know."

"He is—when it comes to computers and human nature—but with something like this"—I gestured at the lockers—"not so much. Have you forgotten about the Dento 5000?"

"It should have worked," Mac said, somewhat indignantly.

your brain. Take a look at this." I handed him the phone.

He looked at the image I'd brought up on the screen, then he looked at me. "Tell me it's not really that color." He was looking at a large armoire painted Barbie pink. It wasn't the first time we'd come across something painted that very flamboyant shade.

"Oh, it's really that color. It sort of glows in real life. What I need to know is can we get it in the back of your truck and then get it off again? It's solid wood and it's heavy."

Mac frowned as he studied the two photos I'd taken of the armoire. "It looks to be about the same size as the one you worked on last year. Am I right?"

I nodded. "It is. But remember that one was in pieces—literally. This one isn't. It has to come down a hallway and then out through a sun porch. I measured everything. It will fit, but there's not a lot of wiggle room."

Mac handed the phone back to me. "We can move it. I can borrow a handcart from Glenn. But I'm probably going to need some extra muscle."

"I don't think that will be a problem," I said. "The guy who's selling the armoire is a big man." I held out both my hands. "And he said he has no problem helping move it. I think he's just happy to be getting rid of it. He also said he had a fair number of phone calls but no takers."

"We're good then," Mac said. "I'm guessing this is for Michelle?"

Given how fast we've been selling dining sets lately it could easily be gone in a day or two."

"What is it with you and orphaned chairs?" Mac asked.

I shrugged. "I'm not sure, really. I like the fact that you can use a chair for more than just sitting on. I like the detail on some of the ones we've found. I can appreciate the craftsmanship. But mostly I think it's Gram's fault."

Mac narrowed his dark eyes. "Isabel is the reason you like to rescue stray chairs?"

I smiled because talking about my grandmother always made me happy. "You know how Gram always has enough food to feed extra people at mealtime?"

"I do." He smiled. "I've always imagined her kitchen is like one of those little cars at the circus that ends up having about a dozen clowns inside, only it's chicken and dumplings."

"Well, if you have extra people you need extra chairs. She'd send me to get a chair or two from Charlotte or Liz and maybe a cake from Rose. Charlotte would make Nick help me if he was around." I laughed. "Which probably explains Nick's love for cake. Anyway, I come across what you call an orphan chair and it brings back a lot of good memories. And speaking of good memories, I really need to get going on cleaning that picnic table so someone can take it home."

Mac had found a child-size picnic table and two similarly sized Adirondack chairs in a free pile by the side of the road on garbage day a couple of weeks dark almond-shaped eyes behind round tortoise-shell glasses. "Hi, Sarah," she said. "How are you?"

I walked across the lawn to meet her. "I'm fine," I said. "How are you and the baby?"

She smiled and wrapped one arm around her abdomen. "According to Dr. Moran we're both fine. And I'm pretty sure I have the Patriots' future kicker in here."

"Wonderful," I said. "We're ready for another Super Bowl."

Rose and Casey joined us. "How are you, sweet girl?" Rose asked.

"I'm just fine," Ashley said.

"And how's Keenan?"

Ashley laughed and shook her head. "It's a toss-up as to who is more protective of me, him or Casey." She gave the dog a fond look. "I swear he knows what's going on."

"Of course he does," Rose said. "He's very smart."

Ashley turned her attention to me. "Sarah, would you keep an eye out for a rocking chair for the baby's room? I haven't been able to find one I like anywhere."

"Absolutely," I said. "What are you thinking of?"

"I'm looking for something . . . old-fashioned I guess would be the best description. What I'd like is a wooden nursing rocker. Something low, without arms and with a caned seat if it's at all possible." She patted her baby bump. "My mother had a chair like that. It somehow disappeared. If I could find something close to that . . ." She didn't finish the sentence.

"I'll do my best," I said.

Casey made a soft whimpering sound then. Rose

Rose glanced at Casey to make sure he wasn't getting too far ahead of us. "I have no idea, dear," she said. "Although I have noticed that sometimes your attention wanders in a conversation."

Out of the corner of my eye I saw Ashley duck her head and try to unsuccessfully stifle a smile.

"Well, umm. I'll try to do better," I said.

"I know you will," she said. She reached over and patted my arm. I felt a little like a six-year-old.

We came level then with the little house. Not only had it been painted since the last time I'd seen it, but the hedge had been trimmed and the rosebushes pruned.

Casey bolted for the backyard.

Ashley sighed.

"It's okay. I'll go after him," I said.

"Is there a tenant at the moment?" Rose asked her.

She nodded. "A man as far as I know. I don't know his name and I haven't seen him but I have gotten to know the rental agent and she said that she had someone coming for a couple of weeks last Sunday."

"We'll go see if anyone is home," Rose said to me. We were just a couple of houses away from where she had been attacked and I felt a little unsettled, but if Rose was bothered at all it didn't show.

I nodded and started down the driveway.

There was no sign of the dog anywhere in the backyard. Where had Casey gone? I called his name a couple of times and then I heard an answering bark from somewhere in the trees behind the house. I cut tapped the screen several times and then turned it around so Rose and I could see. "I saw this at the grocery store this morning."

It was a flyer for a puppy that had been lost yesterday in this neighborhood.

"Do you think it could be this dog?" she asked.

"It's possible," I said. "I need to go lift some of the boards off the opening so I can get a better look." I had a decent flashlight app on my phone. "Stay here."

"No," Rose said in the same agreeable tone she would have used to tell me she liked the color of my shirt.

"What do you mean, no?" I said.

"I mean no, I'm not staying here. Was I not clear?" She looked puzzled.

I glanced at Ashley.

She smiled and inclined her head in Rose's direction. "What she said."

"I don't think that's a good idea."

"Because I'm pregnant?"

"Yes," I said. "The ground is uneven. There could be poison ivy back there or . . . or wild animals."

"Sarah, I know what poison ivy looks like," Ashley said. "Casey and Rose and you are here so I don't think I need to worry about any rogue porcupines, and even though I look wobbly I promise you I'm not."

"I'm not going to win this one, am I?" I said.

She smiled again. "I appreciate your concern but no you're not. For centuries pregnant women have worked on farms and in factories, they've walked miles carrying water and children, they've ridden on horseback and wagon trains and city buses for the opening. I edged closer to the side of the hole. I felt Rose take hold of my waistband.

I used the flashlight on my phone to look down into the space. It was small, probably five or six feet in both directions and maybe eight feet down to the bottom. There was a bag of what looked to be garbage in the corner farthest from me, partly covered with a tarp. A small, wooden ladder was lying on the dirt floor next to a very dirty puppy. He cocked his head to one side and blinked up at me. Then he barked and behind me Casey answered.

I sat back on my heels.

"Is it the puppy?" Ashley asked.

I turned to look at her. "I think so. It's definitely *a* puppy and what are the chances there are two lost in this neighborhood?"

"Can you get him out of there?" She had one hand on Casey's head and I could see the concern in her eyes.

"I don't know," I said. "I can't see any stairs. There's a ladder but it's lying on the ground."

Rose leaned over me for a better look. "It's not that far down to the bottom," she said. "And that ladder looks like it's in one piece."

I recognized the expression on her face. "You're not jumping down there to get that dog," I said firmly.

She squared her shoulders and her chin came up. "I wasn't going to. But you could. It can't be any more than eight feet down to the bottom, which means it would be less than a two-and-a-half-foot drop if you hung from the side."

I found a spot on the rim of the hole where I felt I could get a good grip. I didn't waste any time thinking about what I was going to do. Rose was right. I'd been climbing up, over and under things since I was a kid. I swung my legs over the side and let go.

I landed on the densely packed dirt without any problem. "I'm all right," I called up to Rose.

The puppy barked twice but came to me without any hesitation, his stubby tail wagging.

I crouched down next to him. "Hey, boy," I said, holding out my hand so he could sniff it. His brown and black fur made me wonder if he was part German shepherd. I looked him over but I didn't find any obvious indication that he was hurt. I was hoping he was just cold and hungry.

"Give me a minute and we're going to get out of here," I told him. He wagged his tail again as though he'd understood what I'd said.

I stood up and pulled out my phone so I could use the flashlight and take a closer look at the ladder. It seemed to be nothing more than a makeshift means of getting out of the storm cellar—two lengths of wood linked by several short pieces that made the ladder's rungs. But it was in one piece and looked like it would hold my weight. I leaned it against the lowest edge of the opening. I realized part of the end wall was made of brick. Maybe part of an old foundation?

"I've got it," Rose said after a moment. I looked up and I could see her hands holding the sides of the ladder.

I held out my hand to Rose and she stood up, picking up the puppy at the same time. I helped Ashley up as well and hustled everyone back through the trees and out to the street. We made it to Ashley's little house just as it started to pour in earnest.

"How about a cup of tea?" Ashley said as we crowded into her kitchen.

"I'll get it," Rose said. She gestured at a chair. "Sit," she said to Ashley. She looked at me. "Sarah, could you get both dogs a drink, please?"

I nodded. That rock in my stomach hadn't gone anywhere. "Give me a second," I said. "I need to do something first."

Rose immediately turned all the way around to face me. She'd clearly heard something in my voice. "What's wrong?" she asked.

Ashley looked at me as well. "Something's wrong?" she said.

I cleared my throat. "I, uh, need to call nine-one-one. That bag of garbage that I saw in the storm cellar?" I shook my head. "It wasn't a bag of garbage. It's a man's body."

Chapter 2

"Are you sure?" Ashley asked.

I flashed back to what I'd seen when I'd lifted up the corner of the tarp—a man's body with a large wound on the side of his head. I'd seen a dead body before. I'd known what I was looking at. "I'm sure," I said.

Rose shook her head. Ashley closed her eyes for a moment and exhaled softly. Casey leaned against her leg.

"Just give me a minute," I said. I moved away from them, stood by the door and took out my phone. When I turned around again, Rose had put on the kettle and was getting water for both dogs. I took the dishes from her.

"Right there," Ashley said, pointing to a small rectangle of carpet to the left of the refrigerator.

I set the dishes down and both dogs began to drink.

Ashley got to her feet.

"Take my raincoat," Ashley said. She gestured toward a red jacket on a hook to the left of the door. "I mean it. There's no point in you getting wet when you don't have to."

"All right. Thank you." I pulled on the jacket. The sleeves were a little long but other than that it fit decently. I zippered it up. "I'll be back," I said.

I stepped outside just as a police car pulled to the curb. I walked down the driveway to meet the officer who was driving and let out a breath I hadn't realized I was holding when I saw that I knew him. Like me, Levan Frazier was a runner. He was about average height with the lean build of someone who ran way more often than I did. I pushed the hood of Ashley's jacket back so he could see my face.

"Hey, Sarah," he said as he got out of the cruiser. "You found a body?"

I nodded. I gave him the condensed version of the story, how Casey had been antsy; how he'd led us to the old storm cellar; how I'd discovered the body when I'd dropped down into the hole to rescue the puppy.

"I don't know if there's any connection between the two of them," I said. It seemed odd to me that someone would put up posters for a missing puppy and not a missing person.

Levan gave a noncommittal shrug. The fire department rescue squad pulled in behind the police car then.

I pointed behind me. "My friends are inside with the dogs."

scene van was arriving. She was a detective in the North Harbor Police Department. The fact that she was onsite meant that Nick would probably be showing up soon. He was an investigator for the medical examiner's office.

"Hi, Sarah," she said. "What's going on?" She was wearing a navy police-issue raincoat and her red hair was pulled back into a ponytail. We were standing in the driveway where Levan had asked me to wait.

"Do you remember Ashley Clark?" I asked.

"She owned the dog that found Rose that time she was attacked." Michelle looked around. "Wait a second. That was close to here."

I nodded. "The dog's name is Casey. Rose made him dog biscuits and I drove her here." Once again I explained how jumpy Casey had been and how I'd ended up finding the body.

"Tell me what you saw when you got down there," Michelle said.

It was barely drizzling now. I'd pushed back the hood of the jacket and I rested one arm on the top of my head. "Not much," I said. "I saw the puppy. He was dirty and I was worried he might be hurt. I took a close look at the ladder and decided it should hold me. And I saw what I thought was a bag of garbage tossed in the corner."

"So what made you go take a closer look?"

I'd been asking myself that question since the moment I'd reached down to lift up the corner of the tarp. I shook my head. "I don't know. Some instinct, I guess. Something looked . . . wrong, somehow. But

"No, we didn't. Rose seems to think she has nine lives like a cat."

She smiled. "Considering some of the situations she's gotten herself into—and then out of—I'm not convinced she hasn't."

Rose and Ashley were still sitting at the kitchen table. Casey was lying at Ashley's feet. The puppy was asleep, curled up on an old towel next to the refrigerator. "We called the number from the poster," Rose said. "The same number was on one of his tags. His owners are coming to get him on their way home from work. His name is Dexter."

His owners. So there *was* no connection between the dog and the body.

She got up and poured me a cup of tea without asking if I wanted one. I wasn't a big tea drinker but I was damp and a bit cold and I knew it would be hot. She offered a cup to Michelle, who thanked her but turned it down.

Ashley recounted the same basic story as I had. She explained how she and Rose had knocked on the front door of the cottage and gotten no answer while I had followed the dog. Rose nodded in agreement.

Michelle asked a few more questions, confirming everything I'd already told her, then she got to her feet. She looked from me to Rose. "You two know the drill." We both nodded. She turned to Ashley. "Mrs. Clark, thank you for your help. I may have more questions for you. If you think of anything, no matter how minor it might seem, please give me a call." She set her card on the table.

"I think the hero in all of this is Casey," I said. The dog turned toward me at the sound of his name and I smiled at him.

"I'm sorry about all the rest of it," Ashley continued.

"None of that is your fault," Rose said firmly.

I nodded. "Rose is right. Whoever the dead man is, I hope him being found brings some peace for his family."

I gave Ashley her jacket back and we said good-bye. It was raining harder and Rose and I hurried to my SUV. I started the car and flicked on the windshield wipers.

We drove in silence for a bit. I glanced over at Rose a couple of times. She was staring out the window but not really paying attention to where we were going.

"Why do you keep looking at me?" she finally asked.

"I know what you're thinking," I said.

"Really?" Rose said, her voice mild. "Have you suddenly developed mind-reading abilities?"

I shot another quick glance in her direction. She sat with her spine straight and her hands folded neatly in her lap.

"In this circumstance, yes," I said. "You think whoever that is was murdered and you want to investigate."

"You're very saucy," she retorted.

"Like that's new information to you?"

"That's neither here nor there," she said. "But you're right about one thing, I do think that man was murdered. I'm certain of it."

hand on the steering wheel. "You still don't know who that is and you don't have a client. You're right. Michelle is smart. At least give her a chance to do her job. You can wait a week until we find out who the victim was and how he died before you start thinking about investigating."

What I didn't say was that maybe, somehow, Michelle could come up with an explanation that didn't involve foul play.

Rose made me wait before she answered. "Fine," she finally said, somewhat grudgingly, "but I'm not getting any younger."

"You could easily live another twenty years," I said. "Your grandmother lived to be ninety-eight. Twenty years is one thousand and forty weeks. One week is just point one percent of that time."

Out of the corner of my eye I saw Rose shake her head. "That's what I get for teaching you how to multiply when you were five, though you were so smart you likely would have learned that without me."

"Maybe," I said, "but the cookies were a big incentive."

"I love you," Rose said, "even though you aggravate me sometimes."

I smiled. "Right back at you."

We got back to Second Chance just as the rain eased up a little. In the parking lot there was a woman moving things around in the back of her SUV. A customer, I was guessing.

Mr. P. was in the Angels' sun porch office. They

the boxes in the back of her car." Instead of her usual all-black attire Avery was wearing only black jeans with a white crew neck T-shirt and her usual arm of bracelets.

"Newly engaged, first dinner with both sides of the family," Charlotte said, "and there's no way you can ruin that recipe."

"I've made your beef stew," I said, "and you're right. There is no way to mess it up." I pointed over my head. "Rose is talking to Mr. P. I'm going to get a cup of coffee and put the kettle on for tea. Rose will want a cup."

"Take your time," Charlotte said.

Mac was in the small staff room getting himself a cup of coffee. He handed me the mug instead.

"Thanks," I said. I set it on the counter, added cream and sugar and took a long drink.

Mac reached for the kettle, filled it with water and plugged it in. "You're wet," he said.

I was dirty as well. There were streaks of red clay on my pants and shoes. I raked a hand back through my hair and leaned against the counter with my mug. "It's okay. I have dry socks and a pair of jeans in my office."

"How did the visit go with Casey?"

"It was . . . uh, complicated."

He turned to look at me. "Complicated how?"

"Casey was . . . jumpy. It was obvious there was something he wanted us to see."

"And?"

"And Ashley let him loose. We followed him down to one of the other cottages on the road."

Chapter 3

Michelle showed up just before lunch on Thursday. Rose and Mr. P. were in the Angels' office, and Mac and I were carrying in a vintage metal daybed from the former-garage-turned-workshop. The children's picnic table and Adirondack chairs that I had cleaned up had sold less than an hour after we'd opened. I needed something to put in that empty space. Charlotte had her head stuck in the storage area under the stairs looking for a quilt that we could drape across the back of the bed frame.

Rose must have seen Michelle arrive because she and Mr. P. came in from the back just as Michelle walked through the front door.

"Good. You're all here," she said. She wore black trousers and a gray blazer over a crisp white shirt and black-and-white-patterned knitted vest. I wondered if she might be going to court later in the day. "I wanted to let you all know that the man whose helped her husband fake his death. She has always denied the accusations. She stayed here in town with their daughter and I heard she remarried last year."

Mac's dark eyes narrowed. "Hang on a minute. Ian Stone was from North Harbor?"

Mr. P. smoothed one hand over the few tufts of gray hair he still had. "He was born here. The family moved away for a couple of years when he was a teenager and then moved back. Ian went away to school and he returned as an adult."

"So where has he been for close to three years?" I said. From what I'd seen Stone's body hadn't been in the storm cellar more than a day or so.

Michelle shrugged. "I don't know."

"I think the most important question is was his death an accident?" Rose said.

Michelle took a breath and let it out slowly. "The autopsy hasn't been done yet, but no, it doesn't look that way."

"Who wanted the man dead?" I asked.

Mr. P. raised one eyebrow. "The better question is likely, Who didn't?"

After Michelle left, Mac and Mr. P. filled in the blanks on Ian Stone for me. "Wasn't he supposed to be some kind of investment whiz kid?" I asked as Mac and I moved the daybed into place. Now that I could put the name in context I remembered seeing some news stories about the investigation into the man.

Mac nodded. "He made money by investing only in ethical and environmentally responsible companies.

"So, at some point he and his wife went to Ireland on a vacation?" I said.

Mac nodded. "Stone was about to be looked at for securities fraud at that point, but he hadn't been charged with anything and as far as he was concerned it seemed to be business as usual. He and his wife went to Ireland partly for a vacation and partly to research Ian's Irish ancestry." He looked over at Mr. P. "Weren't they hiking somewhere when he got hurt?"

The older man nodded. "Yes, they were. According to Victoria Stone, her husband lost his footing and went over an embankment into the water. He never surfaced."

"So was there an investigation?" I asked. "There must have been a lot of questions."

"There were," Mr. P. said. "There were a couple of men nearby collecting driftwood. One of them went into the water to try to rescue Mr. Stone. He testified that it was windy and the current was strong. He felt Mr. Stone's body had been swept out to sea."

"With no body, from the beginning there was a lot of speculation that Ian had faked his death with the help of his wife," Mac said.

Mr. P. took off his glasses and removed the little cloth he used to clean them with from his shirt pocket. "But she stayed here in town and seemed to move on with her life over time," he said, cleaning one lens and then the other. "She got remarried. And she always insisted that she hadn't helped her husband fake his death, didn't know he was scamming people

I nodded. "Please."

Together we moved a massive walnut headboard, two nightstands and a dresser that was waiting to be painted. Then Mac carried both pieces of wicker furniture outside while I spread a small tarp on the pavement. One of the chairs was a rocking chair and they were both beautifully detailed with curved edges and wide arms—real wicker, not resin. They were a soft, spring green color—at least I thought they were—and they were both very, very dirty.

"I know what you're thinking," I said to Mac as he stood there, arms folded over his chest, eyeing the chairs.

"You probably don't," he said. "Because what I'm thinking is that I've learned not to second-guess you on this kind of thing because I'm just about always wrong."

I reached up and patted his cheek. "Then my work on this planet is pretty much done."

I mixed up my cleaning solution—a tiny bit of dish soap in some warm water—while Mac started working on the lockers. He had already removed an impressive number of stickers. I should have had more faith in Mr. P.'s vodka trick.

I decided to start on the back of the rocking chair. Because the wicker could warp if too much of the chair got wet, I was going to work on a section of one chair and then move to the other. Happily, the soft toothbrush I'd decided to use was very good at cleaning off the dirt.

Avery arrived just as I moved over to the second chair. She waved and headed for the back door. She

FUR LOVE OR MONEY   47

"Positive," I said. "It's been quiet lately and I like it that way." I looked around and then knocked three times on the arm of the chair.

"What was that for?" he asked.

"I don't want to jinx myself," I said, feeling my cheeks get warm. I really wasn't superstitious—most of the time. "There's no wood here but wicker is close. It's plant based."

Mac laughed. "No, no, no. It's not the same thing. We say 'knock on wood,' not 'knock on plants.'"

I made a face at him. "It's close enough," I said.

In retrospect, it turns out it wasn't.

Liz pulled into the parking lot then and I got to my feet and went to meet her. Elizabeth Emmerson Kiley French—like Rose and Charlotte—had been part of my life for as long as I could remember. She was beautiful, smart and always impeccably dressed. Liz was more than a little imposing and she loved the people in her life with a fierceness that I'd never seen from anyone else. She also believed in cutting right to the chase.

"Are Rose and Alfred here?" she asked.

I nodded. "They were in the office when I came out here about half an hour ago."

"Good," she said. "We're having a meeting."

"We are?" I said. "Why?"

"Because I called one." She made a hurry-up motion with one hand. "Let's go, toots."

She headed for the shop, her high heels echoing on the pavement. "Start moving, both of you," she called over her shoulder. "I won't be repeating myself."

"I don't have a clue," I said, "other than Liz arrived and said she's calling a meeting."

"About what?" There was a bit of an edge to Rose's voice. She and Liz were as close as sisters, which meant sometimes their relationship was just as complicated.

I shrugged. "Don't know that, either. I'm just going to get the tea."

"Are there any cookies left in the tin I brought this morning?" Rose asked.

"Why are you asking me?" I said, a little more defensively than I'd meant to, I realized, as soon as the words were out of my mouth.

Rose gave me a puzzled look. "Because I'd like to know."

Mac was struggling to hold back a smile.

"There are six," I said tightly.

"Bring the cookies, too, then," she said, absently reaching out to pat my arm. Her eyes were on the office and so was all of her attention.

"I'll help," Mac said.

"I'm not the only person in this building who eats cookies," I grumbled as Mac and I headed for the shop.

"Of course you're not," Mac said. It seemed to me his tone was a little condescending.

Charlotte had a large double bed–size quilt spread over the back of a daybed. I recognized her customer. He owned a bed-and-breakfast in Rockland. This was the third time he'd come in and every time he'd bought something.

"Are you satisfied?" Liz said to Rose.

Rose's chin came up. "Thank you. I am," she said. Her tone was just a little huffy.

Liz inclined her head in Rose's direction. "Good," she said. "I called this meeting because Channing owns the cottage where you two"—one perfectly manicured finger moved from Rose to me—"found Ian Stone's body. I take it you all already knew that."

Rose and Mr. P. nodded. Since the body had been found at the cottage, I'd surmised that Mr. Stone was likely the current tenant.

"Why did he buy it?" I asked.

"Sentimental reasons," Liz said. "His mother was born in that cottage. However, Channing has known Ian's father since their college days and apparently the police find it suspicious that Ian was staying there, even though there's no evidence that Channing knew who his temporary tenant was. Despite it being a short-term rental, he's been using a property management company and the thought that he had anything to do with Ian Stone is utter foolishness."

She looked around at all of us. I nodded in agreement. So did Rose.

Mr. P. cocked his head to one side. "Elizabeth, what are you saying?" he said.

She frowned. "What do you think I'm saying? We have to find out who killed the man, of course."

Chapter 4

"Are you serious?" Rose asked.

"Well, of course I am," Liz said. "People are already gossiping, speculating that Channing has been involved in helping Ian Stone avoid the authorities for nearly three years and that's why he was staying at the cottage, which is ridiculous. I won't have Channing's name dragged through the mud, and the best way to stop that from happening is to find that young man's killer and then learn where he's been, who really was helping him and what happened to the money he swindled from his investors."

I wasn't sure I agreed with her logic. Finding out who killed Ian Stone wasn't necessarily going to lead to whoever had helped him fake his own death. However, I didn't think Liz would be dissuaded if I spoke up.

"I'm afraid the last part isn't going to be so easy,"

Liz pressed her lips together for a moment before she spoke. "Thank you," she said.

I could see the wheels turning in Rose's mind. She was already organizing our plan of attack. She turned to Mr. P. "Alf, we need everything you can come up with on Mr. Stone, his business dealings and his so-called death."

"I'm on it, my dear," he said.

She looked at Mac. "See what you can find out that didn't make the news, please—we need to know who made money with Mr. Stone, who lost it, who if anyone might have helped him and who hated him enough to kill him."

He nodded. "I'll get started right away."

Rose turned to Liz. "Find out everything you can from Channing about his friendship with Richard Stone and how the rental of the cottage works. I'll get Charlotte to see what she can find out about Victoria Stone."

"How can I help?" I asked.

"You and I are going back to see Ashley and Casey. She may have heard or seen something she didn't realize the significance of at the time."

"And we can take another look at the crime scene," I said. I knew the way Rose's mind worked.

She smiled. "Why yes, I guess we may be able to do that, too."

"Thank you, everyone," Liz said.

I wrapped my arms around her shoulders and laid my cheek against the top of her head. "Love you, kiddo," she said.

I smiled and gave her the reply she always gave

"I can do that, too," I said.

Rose turned her attention to Mac. "Alfred has a couple of questions for you."

"I'll go talk to him right now," he said. He looked at me. "Are you going to have lunch before you go back outside?"

I nodded. "I'm going to check on Avery and Charlotte first."

"I'll be there in five minutes," Rose said.

Mac and Rose went over to talk to Mr. P. Liz straightened up and had a brief conversation with Rose. Then she stood in the doorway. I realized she was waiting for me.

I needed to check on Charlotte and Avery. "Are you coming to talk to Avery?" I asked.

"I am," she said. "You know how that child is. She doesn't miss a thing."

"Yeah, I wonder where she learned that?"

Liz glared at me but didn't say anything.

There were no customers in the shop. Avery was by herself, rearranging our collection of teacup planters and adding several of the bottles I'd seen her showing her customer earlier. "Hey, Sarah, I sold three of those ugly old vases," she said. "And no, I didn't say they were ugly to the customer even though they are."

"I appreciate that," I said.

Like her grandmother, Avery tended to speak her mind, but she was learning—mostly thanks to Charlotte—that sometimes it was better to keep her opinions to herself.

Avery glanced up at the ceiling. "Charlotte's upstairs looking for a bag. She's taking two teddy bears

I shot her a warning look.

"Which you don't really need to hear."

"If you hear anything," I said, "anything—no matter how insignificant you think it is—you tell me or Mr. P. right away. Deal?"

"Not to mention me," Liz added.

"And don't do anything stupid, please," I added.

The teen rolled her eyes. "Fine," she said. "Is this just your way of keeping me out of everything?"

I couldn't help laughing. It was exactly the kind of thing Liz would have said. "No. Give me credit for being smart enough to know that would never work. There's going to be a lot of gossip about this case. It'll help if we know some of what people are saying."

A customer came in then and Avery went to help him. I linked my arm through Liz's. "C'mon, I'll walk you out," I said.

"Are you sure involving that child is a good idea?" she asked as we made our way back through the workroom.

"No, I'm not," I said. "But one way or another she will end up involved because she loves you. At least this way we have a chance of knowing what she's doing instead of her sneaking around behind our backs." I gave her a look. "It's not that long ago that I was a teenager."

Liz gave a snort of derision. "I remember those days," she said.

I held out both hands. "And look how well I turned out."

Liz just shook her head.

Chapter 5

The rest of the day was very busy. It seemed as though half the bed-and-breakfast owners in the area came in looking for something. Mac sold a large gilt-framed mirror that never made it into the store from the workroom. Avery sold two sets of china and eight sherry glasses that Charlotte had just set out in the morning, and best of all, Rose, who could sell sand in the desert, found a home for a wooden coat-rack that had been in and out of the shop since the day we opened.

Every one of the teacup planters sold. To my surprise something that was just a way to use some of the many cups and saucers we had had become a perennial favorite with our customers. And we never seemed to run out of pretty cups and saucers. "I'll plant more tomorrow," Avery promised. She had a collection of Haworthia plants living on the windowsill in Rose's living room.

backseat, looked up at Avery and licked his whiskers. He was not subtle.

"Can Elvis come with us?" she asked.

I glanced at Rose, who nodded. "All right," I said, "but don't stuff him full of sausage. It's not good for him."

"I won't," she said. She and Elvis exchanged a look that told me he'd at least get a taste of some.

Once I was inside my apartment the idea of grabbing some supper before I headed down to the pub seemed a lot less attractive. I was tired and my shoulders were knotted from moving boxes in the workroom and holding up three different quilts so a customer could get a sense of their patterns. I decided I'd eat down at the pub. I changed into jeans and a lightweight red-and-white-striped hoodie and left my hair loose.

For once I arrived before Jess did. I grabbed our favorite table. Glenn McNamara was nearby with some of his friends, but he came over as soon as he saw me.

"Hey, thanks for the loan of the handcart," I said. "Mac said you let him borrow one."

Glenn ran a hand back over his blond brush cut. "No problem. He said he's going to get an armoire in the morning."

"That's the plan," I said.

"If you need an extra set of hands you know where I am," he said. "I just came over to tell you I'm working on a new recipe—mocha brownies—and I'd love your opinion. Stop in sometime." Glenn owned a

"Sorry I'm late," she said, shrugging off her sweater and hanging it over the back of the chair to my right. "I had a wedding dress emergency. A bride showed up with a gorgeous dress that doesn't fit her with nine days—less than that really—until the wedding."

"Why doesn't the dress fit?" I asked.

Jess sat down, pulling one leg up underneath her. "You know how most of us stress eat?"

I nodded.

"Well, this bride has been doing the opposite. She hasn't been eating because of all the wedding stress."

"So the dress is too big?"

Jess nodded. "It's supposed to be a huge, elaborate wedding that she doesn't really want but her mother and soon-to-be mother-in-law do."

"Ouch," I said. "So can you fix the dress?"

She leaned back in her chair and gave me a sly smile. "Well, I could," she said. "But instead I sold her something I just finished restoring. It's a 1920s wedding dress with beautiful embroidery, a V-neck and butterfly sleeves." She smiled. "And she and the groom-to-be may or may not be setting off on a little road trip just about now."

It took me a moment to realize she meant the happy couple was eloping. I smiled back at her. "So is this going to be a happily-ever-after?" I asked.

Jess nodded. Her long brown hair was pulled back in a braid and she flipped it over her shoulder. "Based on the way they were looking at each other, I think so." She took in the empty table. "Have you ordered yet?" she said.

"He knows that Rose and her crew have a new case. They're looking into Ian Stone's death. The latest one."

She nodded. "I heard it was his body you found."

Nick shrugged. "I talked to Mom. You have to know this is a bad idea."

"I thought you were feeling better about the cases Rose and the others take on," I said. When they'd first started working as private investigators, because their friend Maddie Hamilton was a suspect in a murder case, Nick had almost had a stroke over the danger they were putting themselves into. Slowly (very, very slowly) he had seemed to come around. Rose now considered him part of the team, although he kept insisting he wasn't.

"Not this one," Nick said. "This one is complicated."

"You say that about every one of their cases."

"She's right, you do," Jess added.

Nick glared at her. "Not being helpful."

She wrinkled her nose at him. "Not trying to be."

"So why don't you tell Liz it's too complicated a case for them to handle?" I said.

"Why Liz and not Rose?" he asked.

I shrugged one shoulder. "Ask her yourself." I swiped the last chip from the basket on the table and ate it.

"C'mon, Sarah, tell me what's going on," he said.

"Liz is the de facto client because Channing Caulfield owns the rental cottage where the body was found and he went to school with Ian Stone's father."

"The police talked to him but he's not a suspect. Not as far as I know."

they're doing just because you think it's a bad idea. Because if you don't know that by now, then you're not as smart as I think you are."

"Yeah, yeah, I know that," he said. "It's just that there's so much money and so much deception involved in this case. Not to mention it takes a lot of anger to fracture someone's skull."

Ian Stone had died due to a fractured skull? Was that what Nick was saying?

"Look, I get that," Jess said. "Just give Rose and Alfred and the rest of them"—she shot me a quick glance—"a little grace. That's all."

"Fine," Nick said. He still looked like a pouty six-year-old.

"Did you really give Mr. P. your proxy?" I asked, as much to change the subject as anything else.

Nick looked a little sheepish. "Yeah, I sort of did. It was his idea and it seemed like a good one at the time, though right now I can't remember why. I'd just gotten off of a very long overtime shift. I think it involved something about circumventing a coup should it become necessary. I might be wrong about that last part."

Even he had to laugh at that explanation, and then the band came out for the second set and we put aside everything else.

At the end of the night Nick offered Jess a ride home. "I'm going right by your place."

"Okay, thanks," she said.

He turned to me as he pulled on the hoodie he'd taken off earlier in the evening. "Is there any point in asking you to keep an eye on Rose and the rest of them?"

Chapter 6

The first thing I did when I got home was go retrieve Elvis from Rose's apartment. Avery was still there, sitting at the table in a pair of pajamas that I knew belonged to Rose with the cat curled upon her lap. It was clear she was staying the night.

"Would you like a ride to school in the morning?" I asked.

She shook her head. "Thanks, but I'm going to walk."

I picked up Elvis, who went limp in my arms, all four legs hanging over my arm, his way of protesting me taking him home. Rose handed me a small glass container with two sausage rolls inside. "For your lunch tomorrow," she said.

The cat's nose twitched. "For my lunch," I said, "not yours." He gave an indignant meow.

Rose reached over and stroked the top of his head. "Don't worry," she said. "I'll bring you some sardine

They were both trying to expand the other's horizons.

I smiled at her. "Have a good morning."

Elvis meowed loudly, which I decided was his way of saying the same thing. Avery gave him a quick scratch under his chin and she was gone.

Rose and I climbed into my SUV and Elvis settled in between us. It was his favorite spot to backseat-drive from. He'd watch the road intently and protest loudly if he thought I was driving a bit too fast or following another car too closely. He'd been like that as long as I'd had him and I figured the behavior had to have begun with his previous owner.

We started for the shop. "What did you learn from Nick?" Rose asked when we got to the corner.

I shot her a quick sideways look. "How did you know?" I said.

"You have a tell, sweetie," she said, very matter-of-factly.

"I have a tell? What do you mean? What is it?" I asked.

"You can't expect me to say," she said. "Otherwise I'd lose my advantage." Out of the corner of my eye I saw her make a dismissive gesture with one hand. "The more important thing is what did you learn from Nick?"

"He let it slip that Ian Stone had a skull fracture."

"So someone hit him?"

"Probably," I said, "although I suppose he could have fallen and hit his head."

"Did you see anything down in the storm cellar that he might have injured his head on?" Rose asked.

back of his truck, wrapped in several moving blankets. It looked even pinker than I remembered. With an improvised ramp and Glenn's handcart the two of us managed to get it safely into the workshop.

The piece of furniture was in excellent shape and I had gotten it for a steal. It was going to be the perfect housewarming gift for Michelle. Once she found a house.

I hugged Mac. "Thank you for getting this here in one piece," I said.

"You're welcome," he said. "It's not the only thing I got."

I looked around. Had I somehow missed another piece of furniture in the back of the truck because I'd been so focused on that armoire?

Mac smiled at my confusion. "I got a name."

"A name?" I repeated.

He nodded. "The name of someone who refused to believe Ian Stone was dead and who has been hassling his widow—I guess I should really say his wife now—for the last year. His name is Winston Brown."

"How did that happen?"

"Leon, the guy who sold you the armoire, had his father, Edgar, over at his place. Edgar is a retired teacher."

"I know," I said. "Charlotte is the one who connected us. She knows Edgar."

Mac brushed dust off the front of his shirt. "Well, I don't exactly know how, but we started talking about Ian's body being found and Edgar said a friend of his was one of the man's victims. I managed to get his name without being pushy about it

It was years ago and it was one time as far as she knew. But . . ."

She didn't finish the sentence. She didn't need to.

We stopped at the sandwich shop to pick up lunch. Glenn had everything ready. "Did Mac get that armoire back to the shop okay?" he asked.

"He did," I said. "Thanks again for the loan of the handcart. I'm not sure how we would have gotten it off the truck otherwise."

Glenn smiled. "Hey, anytime. Glad I could help." He gestured at the brown paper bag with our food. "I added three of those brownies for you to try."

"Thanks," I said. "I promise I'll share and I'll let you know what we think."

We ate outside on Ashley's backyard picnic table with Casey at her feet. Rose snuck him bits of chicken from her chicken salad sandwich and Ashley and I pretended not to notice.

"Thank you for bringing food," Ashley said. "It's such a treat not to have to figure out what I'm going to have."

"We'll do this again before the baby comes," I said.

"And after," Rose added.

"Have you heard how Dexter is?" I asked. I'd been wondering about the puppy for the past couple of days.

Ashley smiled. "I had a text from his owners last night. They tried to give me a reward for finding him but I told them to make a donation to the shelter instead. That's why they texted—to tell me they had."

Rose nodded. "We are."

Casey padded around the table to me since no one else was paying attention to him. He laid his head on my leg and I stroked his fur.

Ashley pushed a stray strand of hair back off her face. "Like I told you before, I had no idea who was staying at the cottage. I hadn't seen anyone or spoken to anyone. But if I had known Mr. Stone was there I would have gone and confronted him."

Rose's eyes widened. She looked as confused as I felt. "I don't understand," she said. "Why? Did you and Keenan have money invested with him?"

Ashley stared down at the table for a moment before her gaze met Rose's again. "No. Not us. My sister used to work for a small company in Portland. Part of their pension fund was invested with Mr. Stone."

Rose and I exchanged a look.

"I wouldn't have hurt the man," Ashley continued, "but I would have taken some satisfaction in giving him a piece of my mind." She seemed to want to say more.

Once again Rose reached across the table and caught one of Ashley's hands. "What is it?" she asked.

"I don't want to get anyone in trouble," Ashley said.

"You aren't going to," Rose said. "Something's bothering you. Please tell us."

Ashley nodded as though Rose's words had helped her make up her mind about something. "I told you that I'd gotten to know the rental agent for the cottage."

said. "I left a message and I'm just waiting for her to call me back."

Rose smiled. "Good for you."

We stayed a few minutes longer. Ashley took us inside to see the progress she and Keenan had made on the nursery. It had been painted a pale, buttery yellow. There were white eyelet curtains on the window. And a beautiful maple crib was against one wall.

"Caroline Vega is coming next week to paint a mural on the wall opposite the crib," Ashley said.

"I know Caroline," I said. "It'll be wonderful. And I have Cleveland keeping an eye out for a rocking chair." Cleveland was my best picker. I was certain he'd find the perfect chair for the baby's room.

"We should really get going," Rose said, looking at her watch. She wrapped Ashley in a hug and leaned down to say good-bye to Casey. We made our way out to the car, Ashley waving good-bye from the front step with the dog right beside her.

I drove down to the end of the street and turned around. The crime scene tape was still in place. We wouldn't be getting a second look at the crime scene.

We started back to the shop. Rose was quiet and seemed to be deep in thought when I glanced sideways at her.

As we reached the stop sign at the end of Windspeare Road the silence got to me. "So I guess this means the next thing to do is talk to Winston Brown?" I said.

Chapter 7

"You want to talk to his daughter?" I said. "I don't understand. Why?"

Rose held up one finger. "Because the first thing we need to know is whether or not she ever saw Mr. Stone in person. Clearly whatever paperwork he supplied was fake."

"Okay," I said slowly. "But what if she did see him and didn't realize who he was?"

"Given that the man used to live here and given all the media coverage of his so-called death and other malfeasance, I don't think that's very likely."

I realized she was probably right. I'd spent some time online trying to learn more about Ian Stone. Once I'd seen a photo of him I remembered his face from all the media coverage of his "death." If I'd seen the man alive it probably would have taken me a minute, but I felt sure I would have recognized him.

Rose held up two fingers. "The second thing we

little planters and she was now working on packing the website orders. Charlotte, who had come in early to cover for Rose, was just putting a crocheted lace tablecloth over a black one that was on a dark walnut table with two leaves that Mac had unearthed from the back of the workshop, part of my vow to empty the old garage space before I bought any more furniture.

"That looks nice," I said. "I wouldn't have thought to put those two cloths together like that."

Charlotte smiled. "Neither would I," she said. "It was Avery's idea." She straightened one corner of the lace cloth, stepped back for a look and then nodded with satisfaction. "Now don't panic," she continued, "but we're going to bring in two chairs from your stash."

"Which ones?" I said.

Charlotte turned to look at me. "The two black molded plastic ones."

I knew immediately which chairs she was referring to. They were a flea market find, left at the end of the day probably because the metal legs had been wrapped with zebra-striped duct tape. It had taken a lot of time and effort and several broken fingernails to remove all of that tape and the very sticky residue it left behind.

"I like those two chairs," I said.

"You like every chair you see," Charlotte said. "They're something to sit on, not two kittens."

"Fine," I said. "Just make sure they go to a good home and I want to say good-bye to them before they leave."

she'll be able to use them to figure out who killed Ian Stone." I lifted my head and looked at Charlotte. "Do you think it could be Coach Brown?" I asked. "You're the only one who really knows anything about him."

"I don't want to think that he could do something like that," she said. "He really was a good teacher. He knew his subject inside out and backward and he was good at explaining things and making theories seem relevant to real life."

"There's a 'but' coming, isn't there?" I said.

She nodded. "Winston had a temper, and he was incredibly competitive. He loathed losing. The story about the soda machine was the one that made the rounds, but there were others that were kept pretty quiet about him losing his temper. I wish I could tell you I was surprised when I heard that he went over the line when he lost his money to Mr. Stone."

"But you weren't."

"No," she said. "I wasn't."

Rose came in then. "There you are," she said. "Do you have plans for tomorrow morning?"

I shrugged. "A run. Something with bacon because it's Saturday and then hopefully finish my chairs."

"Could you fit a visit with Kendra Holt into your schedule?"

"I could and I will," I said.

"Splendid," Rose said with a smile. "Ten o'clock." She turned and headed back to the Angels' office.

I wrapped my arms around Charlotte's shoulders. "Do me a favor. Don't talk to Mr. Brown by yourself."

He laughed. "Your dad and I smoked our first and last cigar in one of those storm cellars. Only time in my life I ever saw another human being actually turn green."

"Dad?" I said.

Sam nodded. "Oh yeah. On the other hand, he never smoked another cigar after that." His expression turned serious. "Are Rose and her crew getting involved?"

"They are." Even if I had wanted to lie to Sam, there would have been no point. Like Rose, he seemed to know everything that was going on in town.

He leaned over and kissed the top of my head. "Be careful, kiddo."

"I promise," I said.

Sam clapped a hand on Mac's shoulder. "It's good to see you," he said. "Enjoy your meal." He headed over toward the bar.

"So what is Rose's plan?" Mac asked.

I took my seat again. "I don't know. I never really know. Sometimes I think Rose has some detailed master plan in her head and sometimes I think she's just winging it." I blew out a breath. "In truth, I'd just as soon have nothing to do with this case, but Channing is important to Liz and Liz is important to me. So I'm in."

Mac reached across the table and gave my hand a squeeze. "So am I. And not to change the subject, but where do things stand with that building we were going to empty for Liz out at the camp?"

I sighed. "I don't think anything's changed. With all that Liz has on her plate at the moment, I've been

FUR LOVE OR MONEY   91

to ask—did you learn anything at the poker game last night?"

"I learned a lot of things," Mac said. "The general feeling was that Ian Stone was way too entitled and seemed to think the world revolved around him—good-looking, popular, cruised through school without working hard and spoiled by his father and mother. She died during his first year of college, I learned, and Alfred's friend Merton seemed to think that that was when Stone started to head down 'the wrong road,' as he put it."

Mac tried his fish chowder and made a little sound of happiness. It reminded me of Elvis when Rose made him sardine crackers.

Mac gestured with his spoon. "Merton—who by the way seems to know everything that's going on in town and seems to have a thing for birds, or at least analogies involving birds—said that there weren't that many people in town who had invested money with Stone. According to him, people around here tend to be more conservative with their money. He did say there was a business that went under in Portland, some kind of public relations firm."

"That sounds like the company Ashley's sister worked for," I said.

He nodded. "That's what I thought. It seems the company's owner sued Ian Stone's estate."

"What happened?" I asked, twisting melted mozzarella around my fork. The Black Bear's lasagna was even better than the fish chowder, in my opinion.

"Merton said the suit was dismissed. Something to do with the estate—which was Ian Stone's personal

Chapter 8

I was up early the next morning. It was cloudy but there was no rain in the forecast. It was perfect weather for a long run. When I got back I had a hot shower and then I made a bacon, egg and tomato sandwich. By the time I'd eaten it the day was looking better.

Rose was waiting outside in the hall carrying her ubiquitous tote bag when Elvis and I came out of our apartment.

"Do you have cookies in that bag?" I asked. Elvis cocked his head to one side as if he wanted to know, too. Which I was sure he did.

"No, nosy pants, it's brownies," she said, "and they're not for eating."

"What other purpose do brownies have?"

Rose looped the handle of the canvas bag over her arm. "These brownies are going in the freezer in the staffroom." She pointed a finger at me. "I counted them and I will know if any are missing."

Beside me Elvis meowed loudly. "Yes, I see that truck," I said. The cat was being more of a backseat driver this morning than usual.

I glanced over at Rose. "I'm going to call Dad and see what he knows about Ian Stone."

"Good idea," she said. "You never know where you might find the piece of information that makes everything fit together."

"Speaking of information, what do you know about Kendra Holt?" I asked.

"Very little. Alf says she doesn't have much of an online presence. She worked for a construction firm for several years as a project manager and now she works for this property management firm. According to Charlotte, Kendra is Coach Brown's oldest child—she has a younger brother and a younger sister."

"Why does she think we want to meet with her?"

"To talk about Ian Stone," Rose said.

"And she agreed?"

"Yes." I glanced over at her again. She patted her hair and smiled. "My reputation precedes me."

I grinned. "I have no doubt it does," I said.

Avery was just walking up the street when we got to the shop. We waited for her in the parking lot. Elvis looked up and meowed and she bent to pick him up. Then she looked at me. "Yeah, I know he's spoiled but he's a cat. It's kind of a given." She and Rose *and* Elvis—who almost seemed to be smiling smugly over Avery's shoulder—started for the back door. I hurried after them.

wrist. "Is there anything at all you can tell me about Kendra Holt?"

"What's bothering you?"

"I'm probably overthinking things, but Rose says she told Kendra she wanted to talk about Ian Stone, and Kendra agreed."

Charlotte frowned. "So that's a bad thing?"

"Maybe," I said. "I just don't see why she was so accommodating."

She set down the small wooden bowl she was holding. "I really don't know Kendra, but I've heard two things about her from people whose opinion I trust. One is that she does what she said she would do when she said she would do it. And two, that she's honest to a fault."

"Gram would say those are good qualities to have."

"Sarah, just go talk to the woman. Decide what you think of her and what she has to say."

"Thank you for being the voice of reason," I said.

Charlotte smiled. "It's my superpower," she whispered. "Don't tell anyone."

I mimed zipping my lips and headed upstairs.

Rose and I arrived at Kendra Holt's office a couple of minutes before ten o'clock. The property management company's office was in a lovely brick building about halfway down the hill. There was a woman at the reception desk even though it was a Saturday.

"Welcome to O'Keefe Property Management," she said with a smile. She was probably in her mid-forties with a face that I guessed always looked as though it was smiling.

is my friend, Sarah Grayson. I hope you don't mind that I asked her to come with me."

"I don't mind at all," she said. She offered me her hand. "You own Second Chance, that wonderful re-purpose store, don't you?"

I nodded. "I do."

"That's where I got my kitchen table," she said. "And the dishes I use on it." She gestured to the hall-way on our right. "Let's go down to my office."

Her office was at the end of the hall. It had two large multipaned windows that flooded the space with sunshine. Her desk chair was behind what I was fairly sure was a 1950s vintage wooden teacher's desk with drawers on one side.

"It belonged to my grandmother," Kendra said. She'd clearly noticed my interest.

I ran a hand over one corner of the maple-toned wood. "It's beautiful," I said. "Someone did an excellent job of restoring it."

She smiled. "Thank you."

I looked up at her. "It was you?"

She nodded. "Yes. It's a bit of a hobby." She indi-cated the two mid-century modern chairs on the other side of the desk. "Please have a seat," she said.

I sat down, taking a moment to look around the space. There was a low table under the window that held about half a dozen file folders. A filing cabinet stood in the back left corner and a wooden coatrack in the other. There was some interesting artwork on the walls, including a framed concert poster of Neil Diamond. Kendra Holt was a very interesting person.

"How do you verify a tenant's identity?" Rose asked.

"We use a verification service. We ask for the potential tenant's name, address and contact information, and some form of ID like a driver's license or a passport. In this case we were provided with a passport. The photo wasn't of Ian Stone—I would have known immediately—but I see now that the resemblance was close and everything did check out."

"Did he say what he was doing in town?" I asked.

Kendra nodded. "I didn't ask. It's company policy not to ask those types of questions, but Mr. Cooper"—she stopped and shook her head—"Mr. *Stone* volunteered that he needed quiet and privacy because he was finishing up a book." She smiled. "Surprisingly I've heard that before."

"It sounds as if you don't believe that explanation," Rose said.

"Experience has taught me that it's often an excuse for some kind of an extramarital tryst." She shook her head.

"Had you ever been down in that storm cellar?" I asked.

Kendra shook her head and set the pen back down on the desk. "I didn't know it was there. Mr. Caulfield didn't mention it. Maybe he didn't know, either. I have walked the yard several times but I didn't spend much time looking in those trees at the back. I saw no reason to. As soon as the police let us back on the property the storm cellar will be filled in."

"Does Channing have anything to do with the rental of the cottage?" Rose said.

no matter what anyone said he wouldn't stop. My parents separated over my father's actions. You can ask anyone in my family and anyone who knows me. Heck, ask my father. We've just started talking again in the last couple of weeks."

"Was he ever at the cottage with you?" Rose said.

"Twice," Kendra said. "Right after Mr. Caulfield became my client. Once to help me move a very heavy bed frame and once to help get a trunk that belonged to the previous owner down out of the attic." She looked down at the desktop for a moment and then her gaze returned to us. "If I had known that Dan Cooper was really Ian Stone I would have been the first person to turn him in. Despite what he's done I want to have some kind of a relationship with my dad, and frankly all of this just makes it that much harder."

I believed her. I felt a rush of sympathy for her over what her father had put Kendra and the rest of the family through. And the same way I'd felt grateful because Liam was nothing like Liz's brother, Wilson, I was grateful that Peter, my stepfather, was nothing like Winston Brown.

"Is there anyone else working here who might have been at the cottage?" Rose asked.

Kendra shook her head. "No. Mr. Caulfield is my client. I take care of everything."

Rose looked at me. I gave my head the tiniest shake. I couldn't think of anything else we should ask. Rose thanked Kendra for her time.

"If you have any more questions please let me know," she said.

Chapter 9

I started the car and drove out of the lot.

"We need to talk to Victoria Stone as well," Rose said as I pulled onto the street and headed up the hill. "It would help to find out whether she was being harassed by anyone else other than Kendra's father."

"I'd be surprised if the answer isn't yes," I said.

When we got back to the shop, Avery and Mac were just finishing up with the lockers. They had made short work of peeling off the rest of the stickers. All that was left was for Mac to spray-paint the outside.

Rose and I headed in to talk to Mr. P. He was working on his laptop in the office. We told him about our visit with Kendra.

"I believe her," Rose said. "I don't think she knew who her tenant was and I don't believe she would have told her father if she had." She explained about

Nick spotted me and waved me over. "Sarah, this is Eli," he said. "He's interested in this guitar." The instrument Nick was holding had only been in the shop for a week.

"Oh, very good choice," I said. "This is a Seagull S6, used, but it's in very good shape. It was owned by someone who primarily played electric. The sides and back are laminated cherry but the top is solid cedar. Seagull guitars are made in Quebec. Not really that far from Maine. They're good sound for the price."

Eli eyed the guitar and then looked at me again. "Have you sold any others like this?" he asked. He had dark hair that Liz would have said was due for a haircut. He wore ripped black jeans and a burgundy-colored Henley.

"I've had two other Seagulls and they both sold quickly. I haven't heard any complaints so far."

Nick finished tuning the guitar and to my surprise began to play. I recognized the tune at once: James Taylor's "Sweet Baby James." He smiled at me and sang the first verse and when he got to the chorus I joined in on the harmony without really thinking about it, our voices blending surprisingly well for two people who hadn't made music together in years. We finished and Charlotte and Eli clapped loudly.

"You two are great," he said. "Do you play anywhere?"

Nick and I both shook our heads and I felt my cheeks getting warm. "No," I said.

"You should. You sound great together."

"Got a minute?" Nick said to me.

I nodded. "Just give me a second to get the case for that guitar." The case was in the storage space under the stairs. I handed it to Charlotte, and Nick and I stepped into the workroom.

"Thanks for that," I said, gesturing in the direction of the shop.

"No problem," he said. "It was fun. I'm glad Eli bought the guitar."

"So am I," I said. "I hope he comes to the jam sometimes."

"Been a long time since we sang together," Nick said.

"I'm surprised I remembered the words, let alone anything else." I slid an elastic off my wrist and pulled my hair back into a ponytail. "Did you come to see Charlotte, Rose or me?"

"You," he said. "I'm working on the Stone case. Tell me what you remember about the storm cellar and about finding the body."

"Okay," I said, "but there's not a lot to tell. The ladder was lying on the ground but looked pretty sturdy to me. I figured I would be able to get back up again without any problem and I knew I could jump down." I held up one hand. "And yes, before you say anything, I know I should have just called for help or at least gotten a better ladder."

He sighed melodramatically. "Damn! I had a whole speech about taking dumb chances I was going to give you."

"I'm sorry," I said. I clasped my hands in front of me and tried to look contrite. "You can still do it."

"And there was no way he could *not* offer his opinion on a guitar."

Charlotte smiled. "No. It was good to hear the two of you sing again."

I smiled back and shook my head. "Changing the subject," I said, "Kendra Holt was a dead end. I really don't think she knew Ian Stone was the person staying at the cottage."

"That would have been too simple," Charlotte said. "So now what?"

"Rose wants to talk to Kendra's father and she's hoping Victoria Stone will talk to us as well." ·

"I know where Winston is living." Charlotte reached up and moved one of the Transformers sideways about an inch. "He and his wife are separated. He's renting a little house not far from Alfred's friend Merton."

"The bird guy?" I said.

She nodded.

"Maybe we could take a drive past his house on the way home," I said.

"Take a drive past whose house on the way home?" Rose said behind me.

I jumped and turned around to look at her. "I'm going to tie a bell to you or hang a couple of aluminum pie plates on a string around your neck so I can hear you coming."

She waved away my words with one hand. "I am as stealthy as a cat," she said. "It won't work. Whose house are you going to drive past on the way home?"

"Coach Brown's," I said. "I thought you and I and Charlotte could go talk to him."

*   *   *

Rose left first at the end of the day.

"I have bail money if you need it," I said.

"And I have embarrassing baby photos of you," she retorted.

"Knock 'em dead, Rosie," Mr. P. said.

Greg arrived to meet Avery. The two of them were going to watch a screening of *The Shining* at the library. Mac was going to work on his boat for a while. My Valentine's gift to him had been six months' rental of a large garage where he could finally work on his dream of building a wooden boat.

"I'm only going to work for a couple of hours," he said. "I'll call you when I'm leaving." He leaned his head close to mine. "And for the record, I have bail money, too."

The house Coach Brown was renting was one street over from where Mr. P.'s friend Merton lived. It was a small L-shaped bungalow on a double lot. I parked at the curb and we all got out and for a moment I had second thoughts about what we were doing. We were ambushing the man. This had the potential to go badly.

"There's Winston," Charlotte said, pointing to a man who was working on the hedge on the left side of the house.

Coach Brown was under six feet by a couple of inches, I guessed. He was a solid, barrel-chested man with piercing blue eyes and slate gray hair combed back from his face. He started toward us,

Winston," she said finally. She turned and headed back toward the car. Mr. P. and I followed.

"Poking your nose into other people's business is beneath you, Charlotte," he called after us.

I felt Mr. P.'s hand on my arm. "Don't," he said softly, as if he knew I'd been about to turn around and tell Winston Brown exactly what I thought of him and the horse he rode in on, as my dad would say.

I looked into Mr. P.'s warm brown eyes and my anger faded.

When we got to the SUV, Charlotte turned around to look at her former colleague. He was still standing there with the same aggressive posture.

"And this behavior is beneath you, too, Winston," she said. "At least I thought it was."

Chapter 10

"He wasn't always like that," Charlotte said as I pulled away from the curb.

"He beat the crap out of a soda machine with a hockey stick," I said. "I'm sorry if I'm being judgmental, but that's not exactly the behavior of a stellar member of society. And I get that it's easy for me to say that because Ian Stone didn't cheat me out of a windfall that I could have used to do good things for my family, *but he still had that family*. He still had the things that were important." My voice was getting louder with each word, I realized. Elvis reached over and put a paw on my leg.

I took a deep breath and let it out slowly.

"'Poor and content is rich, and rich enough,'" Mr. P. said quietly from the backseat.

Shakespeare had said it more eloquently than I had. I decided to let him have the last word.

"Then things worked out pretty well for you, didn't they?"

I laughed. We'd had this exchange dozens of times and it always made me feel better. Technically, Peter Kennelly was my stepfather, but to me he was my dad in every way that mattered. My biological father had died when I was little. When my mom and Peter got married I gained a dad, a brother and the family I'd longed for.

"What's up?" Dad asked.

"The Angels have a new case," I said.

"Ian Stone."

I nodded even though he couldn't see me. "Yes. What do you remember about his 'death'?"

"Oh, there was a lot of skepticism that he really was dead. The timing—just as it appeared he was going to be investigated for possible financial misdoing—felt too convenient for a lot of people."

"Those people were right," I said. I wandered into the kitchen and looked in the refrigerator. I had enough vegetables for a chopped salad.

"Yes, they were," Dad said. "But that doesn't mean the people who didn't suspect that Stone had faked his death were wrong. C'mon, it's not the kind of thing that happens very often. It would have taken a lot of planning and a lot of money."

"He ruined a lot of people's lives. There are dozens, probably more like hundreds, of people who could have wanted him dead. And most of them we don't even know about."

"Wanting something and acting on it are two very different things. I'm betting most of the people why Stone came back to town and I'm betting that will help you figure out who killed the man."

"Thanks, Dad," I said. "Love you. Give Mom a hug and tell her I love her."

"We love you, too," he said.

I said good-bye and ended the call. Elvis looked pointedly at the refrigerator again.

I cooked a fishcake and made a big chopped salad with arugula, cucumbers, tomatoes, carrots, dill pickles, cheese and the spicy chickpeas that Avery had taught me how to make and that I still couldn't believe I liked so much.

While I ate I went online to see what else I could learn about Victoria Stone. She'd been consistent in her story about her husband's fall into Galway Bay. She'd married an accountant named Tim Harding almost a year ago. I found only one photo of the two of them, walking down the street, hand in hand. They looked happy.

Mac called about an hour later. "I was thinking, how about we head over to that vegan restaurant that Jess took you to for some of that chocolate cake you liked so much?"

"I think that sounds like a wonderful idea," I said.

"How did things go with Coach Brown?" he asked.

I groaned.

"That bad?" Mac said.

"He refused to talk to us and insulted Charlotte to boot. He isn't going to be any help. What is it Glenn says? We're going to have to do an end run around him."

He nodded. "I remember."

"Fee was one of our new volunteers. She was great with the kids. I think she literally laced up three dozen pairs of skates."

"And how many cups of hot chocolate did you give out?" Mac asked, reaching for his wineglass.

"And how many donut holes did Glenn make?" I said. I smiled. "That was a good day. I hadn't been on skates for years."

"It didn't show. How did you learn to skate like that? The only other people I've ever known who could go from skating forward to skating backward so seamlessly were hockey players."

"That's pretty much how I learned," I said, licking a bit of crème fraîche from the back of my fork.

"You played hockey?" Mac said. "I didn't know that."

"I *sort of* played hockey. Liam was on our high school team, so for several years Dad built a rink in the backyard. You know what Dad's like. He goes all in. The rink had boards and lights and he even built his own ice re-surfacer. Sort of a do-it-yourself Zamboni. Liam and his friends used to play out there after supper." I shrugged. "Some of his friends were really cute. If I wanted to play with them I had to keep up with them. I probably practiced out there more than Liam did."

Mac smiled across the table at me. "You sound like you were a single-minded kid."

I thought about all those early Saturday and Sunday mornings when Liam would be at hockey practice with the team and I'd be on the rink in the

"The principal canceled the sophomore class picnic."

"Classic teen movie plot," I said.

Mac laughed. "Yeah, pretty much. Devin swiped his brother's keys and we got into the warehouse where the flamingos were stored. We covered the lawn of Mr. Haliburton's fancy house in his very fancy neighborhood with those plastic birds and a giant sign that said 'Save Our Picnic.'"

I reached for my wine again. "You weren't exactly subtle."

"Hey, we were sixteen. At least I stopped Devin from blasting '(You Gotta) Fight for Your Right (To Party)' at quarter to one in the morning."

"So what happened?" I asked.

Mac shook his head. "Surprisingly nothing."

"You didn't get caught?"

"Not really."

"A deviation from the typical teen movie plot-line." I raised an eyebrow again. "Interesting."

"We were what you'd call suspects but we managed to sneak Devin's brother's keys back without him ever finding out we'd taken them. And Jameis gave us an alibi."

"Wait a second," I said, waving my fork in the air. "How did you manage to do that? You told me that the two of you didn't get close until you were older."

"Mom and Dad were off at some work party of Dad's. Devin was sleeping over and we were supposed to be playing video games all night and eating pizza. The next day the principal showed up with a whole lot of questions. Mom called Jameis in out, was into the surfer type. Nick wanted blond hair and Charlotte was dead set against it."

"So?" Mac prompted.

"So I told him I could dye his hair blond for him and once it was done Charlotte would come around."

"And how did his hair end up being bright yellow?"

"It wasn't completely my fault," I said, sounding more defensive than I'd meant to. "I tried to get the dye but when I went to the drugstore Rose was there. There was no way I could buy a box of blond hair color because Rose would ask a zillion questions. So I figured blond hair is essentially yellow and I used yellow food coloring, which I think was pretty creative of me."

Mac pressed his lips together, trying and failing not to laugh.

"Nick looked like Big Bird because I might possibly have gotten some food coloring on his skin as well. He wasn't real happy with me."

Mac was laughing now.

"And Charlotte wasn't exactly happy with me, either, because the school awards banquet was ten days away and, as I said, Nick looked like Big Bird."

"And you'd been caught yellow-handed."

I nodded.

"But wouldn't something like that wash out?" Mac asked.

"I thought it would last *maybe* a couple of weeks and fade every time it was washed. Nick washed his hair six times that first day and nothing. He pretty much glowed in the dark." I found myself grinning at the memory. "It wasn't my fault Nick has some

any teen movie. "I think this is the part where the guy kisses the girl," I said to Mac, and then I stood on my tiptoes and kissed him.

He caught my hand. "You said the *guy* kisses the girl."

I shrugged. "Yeah, but I'm a bit of a hooligan."

Mac smiled. "That you are," he said. And then he kissed me. It was definitely a movie-worthy moment.

On Sunday Mac and I joined Cleveland, Glenn and Jess on a hike up to Swift Hills Park. The flea market Jess and I had planned to check out had been canceled. We ate lunch on one of the new picnic tables. Glenn brought mocha brownies. They were as good as the first ones I'd tried.

"I'd hike up here again just for the brownies," Jess declared.

"That can probably be arranged," Glenn said with a smile.

Monday morning Rose and Mr. P. were waiting for me in the hallway. It was raining outside. Rose was wearing her rubber boots with the ladybugs on them and Mr. P. had on his yellow slicker with the hood.

Elvis looked up at me and meowed loudly. I knew I was going to have to put him inside my own rain jacket if I had any hope of getting him to the car in any kind of timely manner.

Mr. P. had updated Rose on all the details of our visit to Coach Brown. "What an odious man," she said, shaking her head. As I'd predicted, she also said we'd just work around him.

help—and with a good cleaning I don't think they'll need to be painted."

"I'm sorry I doubted you," I said. "But what do you mean, you don't think they need to be painted? They're green. Not spring-leaves green or grass green; we're talking I'm-about-to-be-seasick green."

He laughed. "Those lockers aren't the kind of thing that are going to end up in someone's living room. They're for storage. They'll be in a basement or a garage. No one will care about the color. Trust me."

"I do trust you," I said, smiling over the rim of my coffee cup. "Do whatever you think works best. My chairs are done, too. I'm going to make space in here for them and Jess is dropping off the cushions in probably half an hour."

"Sounds like a very productive morning," Rose said.

About an hour later I had the two wicker chairs sitting in the shop. The cushions Jess had made were a medium blue-gray with a winding vine design in a deep green shade that went well with the soft green of the chairs themselves. I stepped back for a look and nodded in satisfaction just as Charlotte walked in the front door.

Rose looked up from the toy soldiers she was arranging on a small table. Her eyes widened in surprise. I was pretty sure my expression was the same. Because Charlotte wasn't alone. Victoria Stone and her husband were with her.

Chapter 11

Charlotte looked at the two of them. "Victoria, Tim, meet Rose and Sarah." She gestured at each of us in turn. I walked over, a little unsure of what to say.

Victoria looked as uncertain as I was feeling. I smiled at her, hoping it helped her apprehension a little. She was tiny, barely five feet tall, with dark hair brushing her shoulders and long sideswept bangs. She had dark eyes and olive skin. She was beautiful. There was no other word to describe her.

Tim Harding was at least a foot taller with sandy blond hair, pale blue eyes and a cautious expression. Under the circumstances I'd look wary, too.

"Victoria came to my house a little while ago," Charlotte said. That explained why she hadn't called first. "She and Tim want to talk."

Rose had joined us. She smiled at Victoria and Tim and somehow the awkwardness in the room eased a little. "Why don't we go back to the office?" she said.

Tim went to stand behind his wife. He put a hand on her shoulder and she reached up and covered it with her own.

"I know that you're looking into Ian's death," Victoria said. "My, uh, former father-in-law, Richard, asked me to talk to you." She cleared her throat. "I know there have been whispers around town that Richard's friend, Mr. Caulfield, was helping Ian. It's not true."

"What makes you so certain?" Rose asked.

She took a moment before she spoke. "First of all, Ian didn't trust anyone." She gave a brittle laugh. "Ironic considering he faked his own death. And second, he would have never turned to a friend of his father for help."

"Why is that?" Mr. P. asked.

Victoria turned to look at him. "Because any friend of his father, especially one like Mr. Caulfield who's known him for so long, would have told Richard. How could they not? And if his father had known Ian was alive he would have turned him in."

Tim was nodding.

"I'm not saying Richard didn't love Ian," she went on. "I know he did. But he also has a very strong sense of right and wrong. As far as his father was concerned, Ian faking his death would have been almost unforgivable."

"I'm sorry to have to ask you this, but did either of you suspect Ian was in town?" Rose asked.

Tim shook his head. "We had no idea."

Victoria let out a breath before she answered and

said. She looked tired. There were dark smudges under her eyes and faint lines at their corners.

Tim gave a one-shoulder shrug. "I'm sorry I can't tell you what channel it was on but I can tell you what time the movie started if that helps."

"Can you think of anyone who would have wanted to kill Ian?" Rose asked.

Victoria closed her eyes for a brief moment. "The police asked me the same question. The problem is I can think of too many people who would have wanted to kill Ian. The people whose money he took. The people who worked with him. The friends who defended him who he made look like fools." She sighed. "The list is very long."

"What about the letters?" Tim said.

"What letters?" Mr. P. asked, pushing his glasses up his nose with one finger.

"Victoria got a lot of hate mail—especially in the beginning—much of it from people who lost money in Ian's investment dealings but also from other people who refused to believe that Victoria hadn't helped Ian fake his death and seemed to think it was their job to tell her she was going to burn in hell for eternity."

Victoria gave her head a little shake and closed her eyes again for a moment. "I don't even have email anymore because no matter how many times I changed my email address the trolls always found me. Everyone seems to think I should have known what was going on."

Tim's jaw tightened. "We still get mail sent to the

that's not what she wants. And she felt that way before Ian did the things he did."

"Fiona is quite a bit younger than Ian—the result of a relationship Richard had right after his wife died," Tim said.

Victoria was nodding her head. "Fiona and Ian were never close. Ian was angry with his father over the relationship he had with Fiona's mother because it happened so soon after his own mother died. Fiona has some kind of a relationship with Richard, but I don't know how close they are. She comes to see Rachel regularly and has since Ian . . . left. I like her."

Tim nodded in agreement.

"How would Ian have felt about his half sister being part of his daughter's life?" Rose asked.

"He wouldn't have liked it." Victoria said. "Before Ian died . . . the first time . . . he wouldn't let her see Rachel. Once he was gone I started letting Fiona visit." She smiled. "Rachel adores her. I'm an only child. Fiona is family. I couldn't cut her out of Rachel's life."

Tim leaned into his wife's line of sight. "Tell them about the fight," he said.

"What fight?" Charlotte asked.

Victoria sighed and rubbed her left shoulder with the other hand. "A couple of days before Ian and I left for Ireland I was in the park with Rachel, and Fiona was there. She was cutting through on her way to her summer job. She genuinely seemed surprised to see us and I never thought us meeting was

Rose glanced at Mr. P., who shook his head. "No," she said. "And thank you for coming to talk to us. I know it can't have been easy."

Victoria reached over and put her hand over Rose's hand. "Please do what you can to catch Ian's killer. If nothing else, Richard and my daughter deserve answers."

Chapter 12

Victoria hugged Charlotte. "Thank you for everything. You're the best teacher I ever had and one of the best people I know."

"And you're one of my favorite students," Charlotte said. "If you need anything, please, please call me."

Charlotte walked Victoria and Tim to the back door and then returned to the office. "I'm sorry to just walk in like that with the two of them. When they showed up at my front door this morning you could have knocked me over with a feather."

Mr. P. was already shaking his head. "You did the right thing," he said. Rose nodded in agreement.

I rubbed the space between my eyebrows with two fingers. I had a bit of a headache. Something about the conversation I'd just listened to didn't sit right with me but I couldn't put my finger on why.

I realized Rose was looking at me. "Is something wrong?" she asked.

"Does it have something to do with the Angels' case?" Jess asked.

"Kind of," I said.

"Do I get to wear a disguise and a wire?"

"No. No disguise and no wire."

Jess made a snort of annoyance. "That doesn't sound like fun at all."

"Will you settle for roasted cauliflower, cake and the pleasure of my company?" I asked.

"Well," Jess hedged. "I do like roasted cauliflower and cake." She laughed. "Seriously, I'd be happy to go with you. How does a vegan restaurant tie into the case?"

"Do you remember Fee from the skating party?"

"I do. Do you remember the jean jacket I redid with the blue velvet collar, cuffs and waistband?"

I wasn't sure how the two things were connected but I did remember. "Yes," I said.

"She bought it and a couple of other pieces. She comes in fairly regularly. So you want to talk to her?"

"I do."

"Okay. I'll meet you there."

We set a time and said good-bye. I had a feeling that going to talk to Fiona Hardcastle with Jess riding shotgun, so to speak, was going to be a lot like doing the same thing with Rose.

Tim Harding showed up just before we closed. He handed Mr. P. a brown envelope. "The more I thought about it, it seemed to me that you should see the mail Victoria gets. Our lawyer kept copies of everything he gave the police. I had him make copies for

footage of Ian Stone but I couldn't see any resemblance between him and Fiona. Her hair was reddish blond and she was lean and slender where her brother was dark-haired and dark-eyed with a solid, muscled frame.

"Good ones, too," Jess added.

"Look, this isn't an ambush," I said. "If you don't want to talk to me, I won't hassle you. But if you're willing to answer a few questions, can we set a time to talk?"

Fiona shrugged. "I don't know how much I can tell you about . . . my half brother." She said the last two words as though they left a bad taste in her mouth. "I don't work until eleven tomorrow. Could I stop by your shop before that?"

I nodded. "Yes. We open at nine but I'll be there by eight thirty. If you come before the store is open, just tap on the front door."

"Okay," she said. "I'll see you tomorrow."

Our waiter came and took our order. Jess leaned back in her chair. "There's no way Fee can be involved in this case. It's not possible. She's a nice person. She's a vegan. She helps raise money for little kids. I've seen her walking a dog."

"She's Ian Stone's half sister."

Jess shook her head. "It doesn't matter. There's no way she killed anyone. You remember the skating party? Memphis was there."

"He brought the sound system."

"Well, Fee stopped him from killing a bug that was crawling up the wall. It was some kind of creepy crawly with about a dozen legs." She shuddered.

a little of each. Both feelings can be valid at the same time."

"I have a question," I said.

"What is it?" he asked.

"Did you notice, when Victoria and Tim were here, every time she was asked a question she paused for a moment before she answered?"

"I did."

"It was almost as if she needed to think about what she was going to say."

"I had the same thought," Mr. P. said. I'd wondered if he had.

"Do you remember what happened when Rose asked Victoria where she was when the murder took place?" I asked.

"Tim said they were watching *Die Hard*."

I was nodding before he'd finished speaking. "Exactly. *Tim* was the one who answered."

"You noticed that as well," he said.

"I think . . . I think it's possible he could have been giving her an alibi." Now that I'd said it out loud it didn't sound as far-fetched as I'd thought it would. I took a breath and let it out. "I'm not saying Victoria has known that Ian was faking his death all this time, but I think she knew he was here in town."

Mr. P. nudged his glasses up his nose. "So do I," he said.

"What do we do now?" I asked.

"I think we need to do a little investigating to see if our suspicions could be correct," Mr. P. said. "Is there any evidence that Victoria may have been at

I nodded. "Okay."

Mr. P. went back down the hall to Rose's apartment and returned a minute later with a manila file folder. "This is close to half of what we got from Tim Harding," he said. "Do what you can."

I took the folder inside and sat down on the sofa. The first letter on the pile had been sent through the mail. It berated Victoria for her stupidity. "I hope you get cancer and die," the person had written. There was a knock at the door. I set the letters on the coffee table. Mr. P. must have forgotten to give me something.

"What did you forget?" I asked as I opened the door.

"So far today, to eat lunch and what I did with my black shoes." It was Nick, leaning against the doorframe.

"What are you talking about?" I said.

"You asked what I forgot."

"I thought you were Mr. P." I opened the door wider. "Come in."

He stepped inside and closer to him I noticed he looked tired. His hair was mussed as though he'd pulled his hands through it several times and there was stubble on his cheeks.

"What are you doing here?" I asked.

"I came to check in," he said. "I just wanted to make sure there isn't anything Rose hasn't shared."

I shrugged. "I don't think so."

Nick noticed the letters spread on the coffee table. "Those are some of the threatening letters and been on the couch between us, on his lap. It was almost empty. Knowing Nick, it could have been the only thing he'd eaten for supper.

"Why are you really here?" I asked. "I'm glad of the company and the help with those letters but you could have called to ask me about Rose."

He raked a hand back through his hair. "Sarah, how long have we known each other?"

I pulled one leg up underneath me. "A couple of days less than forever."

"You know me better than anyone, even Liam."

I eyed him suspiciously. "Do you need a kidney or blood?"

He shook his head. "No. Don't be stupid." Then he blurted, "What's wrong with me?"

I propped my elbow against the back of the sofa and leaned my head on my hand. "So, so many things," I said. "You always eat more than half of the popcorn. You work way too much. You like pineapple on pizza."

I stopped. He wasn't smiling. "Wait a second," I said. "You're serious."

He let out a breath. "Yeah, I'm serious."

"What brought this on?"

"Derek Bradley."

"Didn't you go to high school with a Derek Bradley?"

Nick nodded. "Same guy. He's getting married," he said glumly.

"And that's a bad thing?"

"He has a comb-over. It only has about eight hairs but they're at least a foot long. He's a nice enough guy but he wears his pants higher up into his armpits

I let him stew for a minute while I pretended to think about it. "Fine," I said. "I won't tell them." I offered a pinkie swear.

"I'm not doing that," Nick said. "We're not ten."

"Suit yourself," I said, "but that means my promise isn't legally binding."

Nick shook his head then he gestured at the pile of letters. "If Rose and crew find anything, you'll let Michelle know?"

So we were done talking about his lack of a love life. "I will," I said. "Do you have any idea who could have done this?"

"If I did, the case would probably be wrapped up by now." He yawned and stretched his arms up over his head. "Left-handed people may make up only about ten percent of the people in the world but that still means close to fourteen hundred suspects just here in North Harbor."

Nick got to his feet. I stood up as well and hugged him. "You'll find your pot lid or plate or cookie sheet."

He rolled his eyes, then his expression turned serious. "Thanks for listening."

"Hey, anytime," I said.

Nick said good-bye and I started picking up the letters. So the killer was left-handed. Had Nick let that slip because he was tired, or because he was giving us a clue?

Chapter 13

I decided to head for Second Chance a little earlier in the morning just in case Fiona showed up before we opened. Mr. P. was just coming out of Rose's apartment as I stepped into the hallway. "Good morning," he said with a smile.

"With all that sunshine out there it is a good morning," I said. "Could I drop you off anywhere?"

He was wearing a navy blue Red Sox hoodie and carrying one of Rose's tote bags. Neither he nor Rose was coming to the shop this morning.

"Thank you for the offer," he said, "but as you just pointed out it's a beautiful, sunny day and I'd like to walk."

"Merow," Elvis said, as if he couldn't understand why anyone would choose to walk when they could be chauffeured around.

I was holding an envelope with the three letters Nick had said needed a closer look. I held it out to

"Closing in on three years," I said. "He was hanging around the harbor front and we sort of adopted each other."

"I'm starting veterinary school in the fall. Maybe he'll be my patient one day."

"He's actually a pretty good one," I said. "Probably because he's very social."

Fiona studied Elvis's face. "How did he get the scar across his nose?"

"I don't know. He has some others under his fur but they all date from before he came to live with me."

"You want to know if I killed Ian," she said abruptly, turning her attention to me.

I shook my head. "I don't think you did."

"I threatened him once. Ian was a bully. Technically he was my brother but I didn't like him."

"Did you know he was back in town?"

Fiona shook her head. "There were times when I wondered if Ian could have faked his death, but I had no idea he was in North Harbor. If I had, I would have called the police at once."

She was scratching behind Elvis's left ear. The cat had a blissful expression on his face. He gave no indication that Fiona was lying.

I didn't know how Elvis could tell when someone who was petting him wasn't telling the truth, but he could. He was basically a feline lie detector. The only problem was he'd only take on the role when it suited him.

"Can you think of any reason why Ian came back to North Harbor?" I asked.

I didn't really have any more questions. I thanked Fiona for coming to talk to me. She said a reluctant good-bye to Elvis and promised she'd call Michelle as soon as she got home.

She was just leaving as Charlotte arrived. Charlotte turned to watch her walk past the front of the building. "Was that . . . ?"

I nodded. "That was Fiona Hardcastle."

She turned back to me. "Was she any help?"

"Maybe," I said.

Mac came down as Charlotte started upstairs.

I brought him up-to-date on my conversation with Fiona. "So you don't think she had anything to do with her brother's death?" he said.

He'd made the coffee—the beans were Mr. P.'s latest find—and we stood looking at the spot where my two wicker chairs had been, holding our mugs. The chairs had sold in less than a day. I was feeling just a little smug about that.

"Elvis doesn't, and I agree with him. Nothing about Fiona's voice or her body language made me think she was lying. And what would she have to gain by killing her half brother?"

"Off the top of my head, money," Mac said. "Richard Stone is worth several million dollars. Fiona is his only child now."

I shook my head. "If she was interested in her father's money why isn't she taking any from him? Mr. P. did a little poking around and it turns out she's going to be paying her own way through veterinary school. She has a scholarship. She applied for a student loan and she has some money saved." I took a pulled it off and looked at me. "What do you think?" he asked.

The chair filled all the requirements I'd given him, even the caned seat. It was made of wood without any arms or overly long rockers. The back had beautifully turned spindles. The only problem I saw was that it had been painted an uninspiring shade of brown.

"I know the color is a bit of a problem," Cleveland said, "but I've seen you do more with worse."

I studied the chair. Aside from the color it was everything I'd told Cleveland I was looking for—everything Ashley wanted.

"The color is a problem," I said. "It's going to take a coat of primer and two coats of paint at least. But it's exactly what Ashley described to me." I smiled at Cleveland. "Thank you. I knew you'd come through for me."

He named his price and I didn't dicker because it was more than reasonable. Mac put the rocker in the workshop.

"That didn't come from a chicken coop, did it?" I teased. Cleveland had unearthed more than one find in a chicken coop.

He shook his head but I saw the gleam in his eyes and the way his lips twitched.

I folded my arms over my chest. "Spill," I said.

"Goat shed," he said.

"Goat shed?"

He nodded. "You might want to stick it outside in the breeze for the rest of the day." He was still laughing as he drove away.

Rose smiled and walked over to him. "What are you doing here?" she asked.

He smiled back at her. "I came to talk to you."

Channing Caulfield was about average height but he moved with confidence and that made him seem taller somehow. He had thick silver hair, blue eyes and a ready smile. He wore a gold signet ring on his right hand that I had never seen him without.

He spotted me and that smile was directed my way. "Hello, Sarah," he said.

I smiled. "It's good to see you, Channing."

"Do the two of you have a few minutes?" he asked.

"Go ahead. I can watch the store," Avery called. Most of her upper body was in the storage area and her voice was muffled.

"Hi, Avery," Channing said.

"Hey, Channing," she replied.

"Thank you, Avery," I said.

One arm came out of the storage space and waved in my general direction.

Rose and I took Channing back to the Angels' office.

Mr. P. was bent over a map he had spread out on his desk. He looked up and smiled. "Channing, it's good to see you," he said.

"You too, Alfred," Channing said. They shook hands. "I'm not interrupting, am I?"

Mr. P. shook his head. "You're not." He gestured at the table. "Have a seat."

Channing took a chair, and Rose sat next to him. Mr. P. stayed standing by his desk and I sat on one corner of it as I often did.

Elvis seemed quite content to sit there but I kept an eye on him in case he decided to flex his claws on Channing's very expensive trousers.

"Alfred, do you happen to know when Ian was killed?" Channing asked, turning to look at Mr. P.

"Somewhere between seven and ten p.m. on Monday night," Mr. P. said.

I wondered how he'd gotten that information. Had Nick told him? It fit with what I'd observed. The body had still been in rigor, which meant Ian Stone had been dead less than twenty-four hours.

"Just to be clear, I have an alibi of sorts," Channing said. "I had a meeting Monday night that I arrived at around seven thirty and I left at about quarter after ten. There's a young entrepreneurs club at the high school and I meet with them twice a month."

Elvis was happily getting a scratch behind his left ear and seemed to have no issue with anything Channing had said.

"I suppose in theory I could have killed Ian and gotten to the meeting by seven thirty," Channing added. "But the time would have been tight. I can give you the names and contact information for the two teachers who run the group. They can at least confirm that I didn't show up looking or acting like I had just committed murder."

I looked at Elvis. His expression hadn't changed.

Rose put a hand on Channing's arm. "We know you didn't kill anyone," she said.

"Thank you for your faith in me but I'd like you to check just the same. Due diligence."

"All right," Rose said.

Chapter 14

Rose walked Channing out. I stayed to talk to Mr. P. for a minute. "Was that the official time of death?" I asked.

"It was," he said.

"Where did you get that piece of information?"

He smiled. "My dear, there are some things in life that are better left a mystery and this is one of them."

"What do you think about Channing wanting to hire the Angels to find the money Ian Stone scammed from his investors?"

"It's an interesting proposition."

I smiled. "Very diplomatic."

"Thank you," he said. "I've been told it's one of my strengths."

"One of a great many," I said. "And I think if you decided to take Channing up on his . . . proposition . . . he and Richard Stone's chances of finding that missing money go way, way up."

"We, Sarah," he said. "Not I. The Angels are a team.

the ascot was actually a cloth napkin. The setup looked great.

I decided to stay late to get some work done on Ashley's rocking chair. There were paint drips that needed to be scraped off the seat and back and a couple of spindles that were loose, but otherwise all the chair needed was to be sanded and painted a calmer color.

Liz came to pick up Avery, Rose and Mr. P. They were all going out to supper and as usual the debate over where they should eat looked as though it would continue for a while.

Liz walked over to me shaking her head. "I'm sorely tempted to take them home and give them a grilled cheese sandwich," she said. "Channing said he talked to you all this afternoon."

"He told us that he and Richard Stone are trying to find the money Ian Stone scammed from his investors."

"I think it's a fool's errand," she said, "but they might get lucky. I wanted to tell you that Wilson has reached a plea deal over the furniture fraud at the camp, probably because his co-conspirator—his friend who owns the furniture store they ran the scam through—sang like a canary. He was more than willing to testify against Wilson."

"No honor among thieves," I said.

Liz sighed. "I have come to the conclusion that not only does my brother have no honor, he has no empathy, either. He didn't think about what his

"Bird guy Merton?" I said.

He nodded. "He builds bird habitats—and the occasional cutting board. Merton is a renaissance man."

"He also has all of his own teeth, a rare thing in a man his age and something that's important in a partner, according to Rose."

Mac grinned. "Then don't let on one of my teeth is an implant."

"You secret's safe with me," I said, laughing as I picked up my scraper again.

I worked for about fifteen minutes, carefully scraping away at a long paint drip that ran the length of the rocking chair's left rocker. Finally I straightened up, bending my head to one shoulder and then the other to work out some kinks. "How did Ian Stone do it?" I asked, saying out loud what I'd been thinking about while I worked.

Mac looked over his shoulder at me. "How did he do what?" he asked. "Do you mean how did he fake his own death? Or how did he manage to defraud so many people and get away with it for so long?"

"I can guess how he faked his death," I said. "Money. What I'm having trouble with is how did he scam so many people and get away with it?"

I had an idea about who might have helped Ian pretend to be dead, but I wasn't ready to talk about it, not even with Mac, not yet, even though it was Mac telling me about Jameis providing him with an alibi for flamingoing the principal's yard that had given me the idea in the first place. I had no proof. I might be wrong. I *wanted* to be wrong.

* * *

I'd been home about half an hour when there was a knock on my door. It was Mr. P. "Hello, Sarah," he said. "I seem to be making a habit of showing up on your doorstep."

"You're welcome anytime," I said. "Come in." I stepped back and he came inside.

"I've tracked down the author of one of those three letters Nicolas suggested we look into," Mr. P. said without preamble.

"How did you find the person so quickly?" I asked.

He smiled. "It was more good luck than good deductive skills. The letter-writer quoted René Descartes, among other things. The postmark on the letter and the actual stationery itself also helped."

I smiled back at him. "You know the old saying, 'I'd rather be lucky than good.'"

"In this case luck has led us to Claudia Ryu. She works for a nonprofit in Camden. They raise funds to help children with disabilities go to camp."

"Then it's possible Liz knows this woman," I said. "She's trying to make improvements at the Sunshine Camp so they can work with more campers with physical challenges. I know she's talked to a lot of people already."

"Elizabeth does know Ms. Ryu, who, as a matter of fact, I have an appointment to see tomorrow," Mr. P. said. The expression on his face reminded me of Elvis when he'd managed to wheedle a treat out of me—satisfaction and a tiny bit of pride.

of dark pants and bright sweater. Appearances mattered to Liz and since it was her name that had gotten the appointment with Claudia Ryu I had decided to dress in a manner that I knew Liz would approve of. More than once she'd said, "There's no need to dress as though no one owns you."

As we drove to Second Chance, Mr. P. shared what he knew about Claudia Ryu. She had a bachelor's degree in business and, surprisingly, at least to me, a master's in counseling. She'd grown up in New Hampshire and come to work for Engage Maine almost three years ago. According to Mr. P., Ms. Ryu had streamlined operations at the nonprofit and, even more important, increased donations by twenty-three percent. Writing a vitriolic letter to Victoria Stone didn't jibe with the successful businesswoman Claudia Ryu appeared to be.

When we got to the shop Mr. P. took off his trench coat to reveal a conservative gray suit with a pale green shirt and a green striped tie underneath. I had already taken note of his black leather dress shoes that had been polished to a gleaming shine.

I had settled on a little black-and-white wrap dress with heels that were nowhere near as high as the ones Liz usually wore, but were definitely out of my comfort zone. "You look fantastic," I said to Mr. P.

"Thank you, my dear," he said, "the same is true of you."

"You both clean up good," Mac said with a grin.

"You look very professional," Rose added. She leaned over and kissed Mr. P. on the cheek and then did the same to me. "For good luck."

Claudia reached across the desk to shake our hands and I realized the woman was in a wheelchair.

"You're looking into the death of Ian Stone," she said. She was about forty years old with dark hair in a chin-length bob with a deep red streak in the front. She wore a long-sleeved white shirt with the cuffs rolled back and a wide hammered silver cuff bracelet on her right arm.

Mr. P. nodded. "We are."

"There's no point in beating around the bush," she said. "You must have seen the letter I wrote to Victoria Stone."

"We have," Mr. P. said.

Claudia hesitated for a moment, and I suspected she was taking the time to choose her words carefully. "I shouldn't have done that," she finally said.

I noticed she hadn't said she was sorry.

"You were angry."

She gave her head a slight shake. "'Angry' is too mild a word for what I was feeling." Her eyes flicked from Mr. P. to me. "Do you know what we do here?" she asked.

"Yes," Mr. P. said. I nodded.

On the drive to Camden he had explained Engage Maine's mandate. Not only did they provide scholarships for kids with physical and mental challenges to go to existing summer camps, they also provided grants to various camps in order to make them more accessible to kids with disabilities.

"Then you know that money fuels everything we do," Claudia said. "Almost four years ago one of our longtime supporters died and left us a generous controlled—in the rigidity of her shoulders and the set of her jaw.

"I understand that feeling," Mr. P. said. I knew he meant the words. He had empathy for everyone.

"The police came to talk to me just a few days ago. I immediately told the board what I had done. I know I'm incredibly lucky that I didn't lose my job over this. I have lost the trust of some of the members. And that can't be easily fixed." She exhaled softly. "The police seem to think my wheelchair precludes me from being Ian Stone's killer. I can promise you that if I had decided to kill the man, being in this chair would not have stopped me."

I thought about the backyard at the cottage. I had no idea what it would have been like to maneuver a wheelchair over the uneven ground, but I was certain Claudia Ryu was up to any challenge.

Mr. P. nudged his glasses up his nose. "Do you mind telling us where you were Monday evening a week ago?"

In response Claudia smiled and reached for her phone. After swiping for several screens she handed it across the desk to Mr. P. I leaned sideways for a better look. There were several photos of Claudia in a sleek black dress with a plunging neckline at what looked like some kind of gala.

"The Endeavor Awards," she said. "I was there from about seven p.m. until just after ten thirty. I was upstairs for the rest of the night."

Mr. P. looked up from the phone. She met his gaze directly. "The gentleman with the beard in the first photo?" she said. "I was with him. I'm afraid I don't

Chapter 15

We drove back to the shop. The rest of the day was quiet and when it was over I was happy to sit at the table with Elvis and not think about the case while Mac made spaghetti.

The next morning, I got up early and went for a run. I followed one of the flat routes I ran fairly regularly that passed both the theater and the park. It was such a beautiful morning I decided to do one circuit around the green space. Ahead of me I saw another runner doing the steps at the playhouse. As he turned at the top and headed back down I realized it was Tim Harding. I couldn't remember seeing him out running before.

"Hey, Sarah," he said, catching sight of me as I came level with the stairs just as he got to the bottom. He fell into step beside me. "Are you doing a loop around the park?" he asked.

I nodded. "Yes."

Tim was barely out of breath talking to me and his stride looked good. I told him so. "Hey, thanks," he said. "It's always good to hear I'm not doing as abysmally as I think."

"The first time I went running I thought I was doing so well and then I tripped over my own shoe lace," I said.

"You're not serious," he said.

"Sadly, I am," I said with a smile. I was watching his hands, looking for any sign that he was a lefty or a righty and wishing I had paid attention when he was writing his lawyer's name on the envelope of letters he'd dropped off.

"I'm going to do another circuit," Tim said as we approached the park entrance again.

"And I'm heading back," I said, gesturing to the right.

"Thanks for the company," he said. "I hope I see you out here again."

"Me too," I said. I turned toward the sidewalk and Tim raised a hand in good-bye. His right hand. I wondered if that meant anything.

I ran home, had a very hot shower and made scrambled eggs with spinach and a piece of sourdough toast.

Mr. P. was waiting in the hallway as usual, once again wearing his Red Sox hoodie and carrying Rose's tote bag. "Good morning," he said. "Rosie will be right out. She's taking a phone call from Tabitha."

I glanced down the hall at her apartment door. "I

when she made a note at the reception desk. Hand-edness is genetic so maybe her father is left-handed as well."

"Victoria Stone may be," Mr. P. said. "I noticed she was playing with a pen that was on the table while we were talking. She used her left hand."

"Charlotte may know," I said. Out of the corner of my eye I saw Rose nod in agreement.

"By the way, I shared our suspicions about Victoria with Rosie," Mr. P. added.

I flicked another glance in Rose's direction. "What do you think?" I asked.

"I'd like to think you're wrong," she replied. "But past experience tells me that would be a mistake."

"So what should we do?"

"I'm going to need to think about that," she said.

I nodded. "Okay." I glanced in the rearview mirror again. "What about Tim Harding? Do you have any idea whether he's right- or left-handed?"

"Tim Harding is definitely right-handed," Mr. P. said. "When he wrote down his lawyer's name he used his right hand."

"I'm glad you were paying attention," I said. "Because I couldn't remember."

"Channing is right-handed," Rose said. "I'm certain of that. Not that he was ever a suspect."

"Even so, I take it his alibi checked out."

"It did," she said.

"So all we need to do is find out if the coach is left-handed."

"Merow!" Elvis said.

the coach used to have the team run the trails in that part of town and all the way up to Swift Hills as well. That means he knew the area. Maybe, I don't know, maybe he was there and somehow saw Ian." I sighed. "That made more sense when I was just thinking it."

Mr. P. was already shaking his head. "No, my dear, it makes a great deal of sense. I've been digging into Coach Brown. Not an easy task, by the way, because he has no social media presence. But I did learn a few things. He's going to be coaching at a summer hockey camp and he takes on some private students to get them ready for that same camp."

"So he could have had those students out running on the same trails he used to have his high school hockey players training on."

"Yes, he could."

"He could have seen Ian," I said. "It *is* possible. Dumb luck, but possible."

"'When you have eliminated all which is impossible, then whatever remains, however improbable, must be the truth.'" Mr. P. smiled as he quoted Sherlock Holmes.

"Has Rose heard from Kendra?" I asked.

"As far as I know, she hasn't," he said.

"So until Rose decides what we should do about Victoria Stone and we find out whether or not the coach is left-handed, we're stuck."

Mr. P. smiled. "Not necessarily. I have an idea. It has to do with robots. I just need a little more time to do a bit more digging."

Chapter 16

Kendra called Rose about an hour later. If she was curious about why Rose wanted to know if her father was left-handed it seemed she didn't ask. "And yes, Winston Brown is left-handed," Rose said.

So based on what Nick had told me Coach Brown could have killed Ian Stone. Of course so could the other 1,399 or so left-handed people in North Harbor. Not to mention the remaining two of the three letter-writers Nick had suggested we check out, assuming any of them were left-handed. The whole thing gave me a headache.

When Charlotte arrived at lunchtime she confirmed that Victoria Stone was also a lefty.

"Winston Brown. Kendra Holt. Victoria Stone." I counted them off on my fingers. "What are the chances three people connected to this case would all be left-handed just the way the killer is?" I asked.

Mr. P. tipped his head to one side and thought about

"Could you come inside for a minute, please?" he said. "I'm sorry to take you away from your work."

"It's all right," I said. "I don't mind."

I followed him inside to the office. I leaned against the doorframe. He stood by his desk.

"When we went to see the coach did you pay much attention to what he was doing?" Mr. P. asked.

"He was doing yard work. He had hedge clippers and I'm pretty sure I saw a leaf blower." I wasn't sure where we were going but I knew Alfred Peterson did not run off on a metaphorical goose chase.

"Exactly," he said, smiling as though he was the teacher and I was his prize student. "Very expensive, top-of-the-line hedge clippers with a solar panel charger, along with an equally expensive leaf blower *and* a robot lawnmower. Again, one of the best money can buy."

So that's where the robot came in.

"How did he pay for it all?" Mr. P. asked.

"I, uh, I don't know," I said. "A credit card, probably."

"That's a two-thousand-dollar lawnmower," he said.

I stared at him. "Seriously?"

He nodded. "There were several thousand dollars' worth of lawn equipment in that yard. The yard of a man who is separated from his wife. A teacher's pension doesn't go that far. So I checked out the man's finances." The gleam in his eye told me he'd found something.

"And?" I prompted.

"He has an account with an online bank that is in

we headed out the back door. I was glad someone did because I wasn't sure I did.

"I'm just going to let Mac know where we're going," I said. I handed Mr. P. my keys.

"You two going somewhere?" Mac asked as I walked up to him.

"We're going to talk to Winston Brown again," I said. "Or at least try to. It looks like he might have been blackmailing Ian."

Mac shook his head. "Because that kind of thing always turns out so well," he said. "I should come with you."

"That would leave Rose by herself," I said. "Avery won't be here until later. She has a meeting at school. Remember? And there's nothing to worry about anyway."

"What do you mean 'nothing to worry about'? You just said Brown might have been blackmailing a man who turned up dead?"

I nodded. "Exactly. Blackmailing. Not murdering."

He frowned. "So you don't think he killed Ian after all?"

"It strikes me that an alive Ian Stone was worth way more to the coach than a dead one."

He caught my hand and gave it a squeeze. "Just be careful, please?"

"I will," I said.

When we got to the former teacher's house it turned out he wasn't home. "We could wait for a little while," I said to Mr. P. "Or come back later."

stance. I studied the man's demeanor, trying to figure out how he could be Kendra's father. Finally after half a dozen balls—none of which went into the
cup—he looked up at us. "Still not talking to you,"
he said.

"Oh, you don't have to talk to us," Mr. P. said. "We
came to talk to you. We know you were blackmailing Ian Stone."

The former teacher stiffened. "That's ridiculous,"
he said. His gaze slid off to one side.

Mr. P. stood with his hands folded in front of him.
"What I find ridiculous is that a man with your education and experience did such an appalling job of
hiding the money Mr. Stone gave you. That does not
say good things about the way our education system
teaches critical thinking."

I didn't think the fact that Coach Brown was a
lousy thief was the fault of the school system, but it
didn't seem like a good time to question Alfred's
logic.

Mr. Brown was still holding his club. He set another golf ball on the turf. "If you don't stop harass-
ing me I'm calling the police," he said. He tapped the
ball and it hooked to the right the way all the previous ones I'd seen had done. I didn't really know anything about the sport but there was something odd
about both his stance and his putting.

"What a splendid idea," Mr. P. said. "I can make
the call if you'd rather." He pulled out his phone and
held it up.

That was enough to get Coach Brown to look directly at him. Mr. P. held his gaze without flinching.

is left-handed. It's just wasn't Coach Brown. He wouldn't have been able to generate the force."

I leaned back against the seat, closed my eyes for a moment and shook my head. "We just lost our best suspect."

Chapter 17

"I wish it weren't the case," Mr. P. said.

"Have you had any luck finding any security camera footage from Windspeare Point?" I asked.

"If all goes well I should have footage from two different cameras waiting in my inbox."

"Then let's head back and see what's there," I said.

We drove back to Second Chance. There was a woman in the parking lot moving things around in the backseat of an SUV. Mr. P. went to his office to call Michelle. I went into the shop to find Rose packing up a set of Liberty Blue China for a customer who had also bought two sets of silver-edged cordial glasses.

I wrapped the glasses while Rose explained to me that the woman, who I guessed was in her late forties, was going to be hosting afternoon tea for her mother-in-law's birthday. The mother-in-law had once owned a set of Liberty Blue dishes. The dishes had been a promotional grocery store giveaway and

"Kendra? I don't think so."

His dark eyes narrowed. "You don't think so because there's no evidence to support that idea? Or you don't think so because you liked her."

I linked my fingers together behind my head. "I do like Kendra," I said. "And as far as I know there's no evidence that she killed Ian, other than the fact that she's left-handed, although physically she could have done it."

"So where was she when the murder took place?"

I thought for a moment. "I don't know," I said slowly. "Rose didn't ask the question because when we went to talk to Kendra we were looking for information about her father." I grimaced. "We're going to have to ask that question, aren't we?"

He nodded. "I think you are."

"We still have two of those three people Nick singled out who wrote those threatening letters to Victoria," I said. I stretched both arms over my head then dropped them to my sides. "I know Mr. P. is doing some more digging into both of them."

Mac had a thoughtful expression on his face. "What about Tim Harding?" he asked. "From what you said he's very protective of his wife. And are they legally married since Ian Stone was actually alive when their marriage took place?"

I shook my head. "You'll have to ask Mr. P. about that last part. As for Tim being the one who killed Ian, it's not possible. He's right-handed."

"What about Victoria?" Mac asked.

"She certainly had motive," I said. "She's left-handed, and I think she knew Ian was in town. But

had were sticking straight out from the sides of his head.

I stared down at the letter. "Why does that name feel familiar?" I said, more to myself than Mr. P.

"I don't know," he replied, "since Herbert Charlemagne seems to be as insubstantial as a wraith."

I closed my eyes and put one hand on the top of my head as though I could somehow push what I was looking for out of my brain. "Herbert Charlemagne," I repeated to myself, and after a moment I could hear my mother's voice in my head saying that name.

I opened my eyes and gestured at Mr. P.'s laptop. "May I?" I asked.

"Of course," he said. He looked curious but didn't ask me what I was doing.

After a couple of moments at the keyboard I turned the laptop around so Mr. P. could see the screen. It showed a children's book from the library's collection.

"Herbert Charlemagne is the main character in a series of children's books from the 1950s," I said.

"So I was correct that this letter writer was using a pseudonym."

I nodded.

"And we seem to have reached an impasse."

"I don't think so," I said.

Mr. P. frowned. "Why do you say that?" he asked.

I sat on the corner of the desk. "My mother has all six books in the series."

"That doesn't surprise me since she is a children's

"Sometimes the long shot pays off," he said. "Look at Donerail."

"I'd be happy to if I knew who or what Donerail is," I said. "My first guess would be some kind of epic battle in Ireland about five hundred years ago."

Mac made a face. "Not even close. Donerail is the biggest long shot to ever win the Kentucky Derby."

"A horse," I said.

He smiled. "A very good horse. It was back in 1913 and the odds were ninety-one to one. If Donerail can win the Derby why can't the odds work in your favor?" He held up one hand and I half expected him to say "ta-da" or something similar.

"Your pep talks need a little work," I said, "but this one will do. We won't be long."

"Do you know Marta Brooks?" Mr. P. asked as we walked in the main doors at the library.

"I know her by sight," I said, "and we've spoken a couple of times."

I decided the fastest way to find the librarian was to ask at the reference desk. We were directed to the kids' picture book section, where Marta was shelving.

"That's her," I said to Mr. P.

Marta was in her twenties, tall, with a mass of blond curly hair. She was wearing a red dress along with red tights that had little yellow ducks all over them. We walked over to her and I introduced myself and Mr. P.

"We're looking into the death of a man named Ian Stone," Mr. P. said.

She nodded. "Yes."

"Do you mind telling us where you were last Monday night?" Mr. P. asked.

Marta looked a bit sheepish. "I was axe throwing with some of my friends. There are photos on my Facebook page."

"I'd like to try that," Mr. P. said. "Is it difficult?"

"It wasn't as hard as I expected," she said. "The trick is to keep the axe straight. Don't let it lean right or left."

Mr. P. nodded and I had the feeling we'd all be going axe throwing sometime soon.

"I should talk to the police, shouldn't I?" Marta said.

"I think that would be a good idea," I said.

"Talk to Detective Andrews," Mr. P. added.

Marta promised she would and Mr. P. thanked her for talking to us.

"Is it wrong to want to whack Winston Brown over the head with an atlas?" I asked as we made our way through the library toward the main doors.

Mr. P. smiled. "As long as you don't actually do it, it's okay to want to," he said.

Rose was alone in the shop dusting a tall dresser when we got back. "Well?" she asked.

I shook my head. "We've eliminated another letter writer, and by the way, Winston Brown couldn't have killed Stone, either. However, he was black-mailing him. Mr. P. can give you the details."

"Well, that's unfortunate," she said. "He was our prime suspect."

Greg by the arm, all but dragging him with her through the door to the workroom.

Rose looked from the two chairs to the round table. "She's right," she said. "The two types of wood don't really jibe and neither do the two styles."

I made a face. I liked the two oak chairs a lot less than I did the two Windsor chairs, which I was guessing Avery had gone to get.

I was right. Avery and Greg came back with the two chairs and she set them on either side of the table. They did look a lot better.

"See?" she said to me.

"I see. You're right," I said. I put a hand on the back of one of the oak chairs. "So what would you do with these two?"

Avery looked around the room, turning in a slow circle. "You sold the suitcases," she exclaimed after a moment.

"Rose did," I said.

"Excellent."

"All the credit is yours," Rose said with a smile. "They sold because someone noticed them in the window."

Avery smiled back at her then she looked at me again. "Sarah, where's that orange foot stool thing?" she asked.

"It's out in the workroom underneath the shelves on the back wall. It's wrapped in a pink flowered sheet," I said. "Why?"

She frowned, her nose wrinkling. "And is that black lacquer tray still under the stairs?"

I watched Greg moving a quilt rack for Avery. I remembered that he was a movie buff. "Greg, do you know much about the movie *Die Hard*?" I asked. I knew the film starred Bruce Willis but I'd never seen it.

Avery rolled her eyes. "It's only one of his favorite movies." She looked at him. "And for the record, *not* a Christmas movie."

"*Die Hard* is one of the greatest action films of all time," Greg said. "Bruce Willis, Alan Rickman, Bonnie Bedelia. Both Sylvester Stallone and Arnold Schwarzenegger turned down the role of John McClane." His eyes narrowed. "You haven't seen it?"

I shook my head. "Never."

Avery nudged him with her hip. "See?" she said. "Not everyone thinks it's the best movie ever."

"So do you at least know the storyline?" Greg asked.

"Sort of," I said. "Bruce Willis is a New York City police detective. He and his wife are separated or something but he's going to meet her at her company Christmas party because he wants them to get back together. Then terrorists take over the building and Bruce's character has to save his wife and take down the bad guys."

"You've pretty much got it," he said. "The bad guys are not really terrorists. They're after millions of dollars of untraceable bearer bonds that are in a safe in the building." He frowned. "What are you trying to find out? It has to do with someone you're all investigating, doesn't it?"

I glanced at Rose, who nodded. "It does," I said. "I think someone only pretended to watch *Die Hard*

Chapter 18

"I'm not sure we have enough evidence to make that conclusion," Rose said.

"But I could be right," I said.

She nodded. "It's possible."

I recognized the irony in the conversation we were having. Usually it was Rose making leaps of logic and me trying to rein her in.

"We need to talk to Victoria when Tim is not around," she continued.

"How are we going to do that?"

"We should to talk to Alf," Rose said. She led the way back through the shop. "Can you handle things here for a few minutes?" she said to Avery, who was rearranging the small glass bottles I'd set on the table.

"Yeah, I've got this," she said.

Mr. P. was working on his computer. A black-and-white video was playing on the screen at what looked to be at least double speed. He paused the playback.

led me to a chat room and someone named Pounder314. It turns out that Pounder314 is the username of Ted Fleming. He lives here in North Harbor."

"Are we going to talk to him?" I asked.

"I think we should," he said.

We decided on an unannounced visit at the end of the day.

"Mr. Fleming—it seems his friends call him Pounder—is a bit of a conspiracy theorist," Mr. P. explained. "Among other things he seems to think Earth is flat."

"If Earth is flat why haven't the oceans all drained away by now?" I asked.

Mr. P. smiled. "I think that's a question best posed to Mr. Fleming."

It was quiet at Second Chance for the rest of the afternoon so I had lots of time to wonder how Mr. P. was going to get Tim away from his house. Even though he had promised not to break any laws, that didn't mean he might not stretch a few.

The three of us—along with Elvis—drove out to Ted Fleming's house at the end of the day. He lived close to Glenn's uncle and I was confident I could find the place with Mr. P. supplying the directions.

Mac already had plans. "I think I'm going to be sorry I missed this little excursion," he said.

On the way Rose brought us up-to-date on what was happening with her friend Tabitha and the residents' committee Tabitha was organizing at Legacy Place.

"Tabitha is beginning to suspect building management is just paying them lip service, pretending

to him I saw that it seemed to be lined with aluminum foil.

It was definitely a bad idea to come here unannounced, I thought.

"Are you from the government?" he asked.

Mr. P. shook his head. "I'm a private detective."

Fleming, assuming it was him, frowned. "You don't look like one."

Mr. P. was unfazed. "What does a private detective look like?" he asked.

"Thomas Magnum, P.I.," Fleming replied at once. "The original, not the retread."

Mr. P. nodded in agreement.

Fleming pointed at me. "She your secretary?"

Before I could answer, Mr. P. said, "Yes."

"Where's her notepad?"

Mr. P. pulled a small notebook and a pen from his jacket pocket and handed them to me.

The younger man folded his arms over his chest. "What's your case?" he asked.

"The murder of Ian Stone," Mr. P. replied.

"The man who died twice."

Alfred nodded. "You wrote his wife a letter."

Fleming's blue eyes narrowed. "How do you know?" he said.

"I'm sorry," Mr. P. said. "I can't reveal my source."

"Yes, I wrote Mrs. Stone a letter. Her husband took my money. You can't take things that don't belong to you. She may be an android. I'm not sure."

I glanced back over my shoulder and saw Rose approaching.

Ted Fleming pointed at me. "Is she an android?"

very well so I sort of decided if I seemed a little, well, crazy, maybe I could sell more."

He looked from Rose to Mr. P. and me. "There's a lot of people out there that think the government and some of those big computer companies are doing some shady things." Ted—Eddie, I wasn't sure how to think of him now—shrugged. "And for all I know maybe they are. What I know for sure is once it seemed like I was one of them, they bought my books."

"Shame on you," Rose said, shaking her head.

"I didn't hurt anyone," he protested.

"Really?" she said.

"What about Victoria Stone?" Mr. P. asked.

Fleming vigorously shook his head. "I didn't hurt her. I didn't go anywhere near her. Yeah, I wrote her a letter, but just to scare her in case she knew where her husband's money was because some of it was my money. And I might have been a little drunk or maybe a lot drunk at the time."

Rose sighed. "Eddie Fleming, you are better than that."

"I'm not so sure about that, Mrs. Jackson," he said, shaking his head.

"Well, I am," she stated firmly. "Where were you on Monday night last week?"

"Same place I am every Monday night," he said. "Online in a UFO chat room. Last week everyone was talking about the UFO that people saw last month."

"That wasn't a UFO, it was a meteorite," Mr. P. said.

"Yeah, I know that," Fleming said. He shrugged.

woman whose chest seemed about to fall out of her dress. The book's title was *The Earth Moved*.

"Yes, I know it probably has a lot of sex in it," Rose said in a matter-of-fact tone. "That doesn't mean I can't judge what kind of writer Eddie is. He always had a very vivid imagination."

"Okay," I said. I started the car. I did *not* look in the rearview mirror at Mr. P.

I went to the jam hoping that Eli, the young man Nick had sold the guitar to, would show up, but he didn't. As usual, Sam and the guys were wonderful and I left with my brain a little more settled.

Rose and I *and* Elvis were sitting in my SUV the next morning at quarter to eight. Elvis had refused to stay in our apartment and I didn't have the time to argue with him.

Rose's phone rang at five minutes to eight. She answered, looked at me and nodded. I started the car and we were pulling out of the driveway before she'd finished talking to Mr. P.

"Make sure you stay within the speed limit," Rose warned.

Elvis meowed his agreement.

"I would hate to have this whole endeavor derailed."

"I will obey all speed limits and posted signage," I said primly.

"A new driving experience for the both of us," Rose said, sotto voce, to the cat.

kitchen. It was on the left side of the house, its windows overlooking the driveway. "Please have a seat," she said, indicating the table and four chairs in front of the windows.

I ran my hand over the top of the chrome table. It was a deep rosy pink. "This is beautiful," I said.

Victoria smiled. "It is, isn't it? It used to belong to Tim's grandmother. She gave it to us when we got married." She took three china mugs down from a cupboard above the sink. "I guess we're not really married since Ian wasn't actually dead."

"That can be easily remedied," Rose said. Her gaze flicked to me for a brief moment. "How did you find out he was still alive?"

The color drained from Victoria's face. She set the teapot that she had just picked up back down again. Rose got to her feet and pulled out the empty chair between us. She touched Victoria's arm. "Come sit," she said.

Victoria sat down. She swallowed a couple of times as though there was a lump in the back of her throat she couldn't get down. Then she wrapped her arms around herself. "I . . . I didn't know Ian had faked his death. I know a lot of people thought I did but I swear to you I didn't."

"How did you find out he was alive?" Rose asked again. She looked at me and tipped her head toward the teapot.

I got to my feet and poured a cup for each of us. I found spoons in a nearby drawer. The sugar bowl was already on the table and there was milk in the asked me to if anything happened to him. I told him I would bring them to him."

Rose leaned forward in her chair. Her eyes never left Victoria's face. "Did he tell you where he was staying?"

Victoria shook her head. "He asked me to meet him back at the park Monday morning. I don't know why I said yes." She looked at Rose. "I really don't."

"You loved him once," Rose said. "He's your daughter's father."

"I did love him at one time," Victoria said. "Maybe that's why I didn't call the police. I don't know."

"So you met Ian at the park," Rose said. "What happened?"

"He kissed me. And he said Rachel and I could come with him. I told him I needed to think about it but I knew I couldn't do that to Rachel. She deserves to have a normal life and she adores Tim. And so do I. He's kind and loving and he would never, ever do something like pretend to be dead."

I noticed how tiny Victoria was, no bigger really than Rose, who was barely five feet tall in her sensible walking shoes. How could she have killed Ian and dumped his body in the storm cellar? She had to be more than a foot shorter than he was. The height difference alone was a problem.

Victoria put both hands flat on the table. "I didn't kill Ian," she said. She looked at Rose and then at me. "I know you don't have any reason to believe me, but I swear I didn't."

"Where were you the night Ian died?" I asked. "You weren't watching *Die Hard*, were you?"

"I know," Victoria said. "Are you going to tell them?"

"It's not my story to tell," Rose said. "But I think you need to think about telling them."

She sighed. "I . . . I don't know if I can do that. They're going to think that if I lied about that maybe I lied about killing Ian as well."

Rose gave her a sympathetic smile. "In my experience, Detective Andrews is not the kind of person who jumps to conclusions."

She got to her feet and I stood up as well. She put a hand on Victoria's shoulder for a moment. "Be good to yourself," she said.

Victoria nodded.

We walked back to the car. Elvis was in the middle of the front seat, dozing in a patch of sunshine. As soon as we pulled away from the house Rose sent Mr. P. a text.

I felt the knot that had settled in the pit of my stomach begin to let go. I glanced over at Rose. "Do you believe her?" I asked.

She sighed. "I think so," she said. "Why would she admit to having been in contact with her former husband if she *had* killed him? That just makes her look more guilty."

"I had the same thought," I said, "and I'm not sure she's physically capable of dumping his body in that storm cellar."

"She could have lured him down there," Rose said. Out of the corner of my eye I saw Elvis stretch and sit up. Rose reached over to stroke his fur.

"She could have," I agreed. "But she still had to

Chapter 19

It felt as though we'd spent a long time with Victoria, but in reality we hadn't. We were actually a little early getting to the shop. Mac had made coffee and I was happy to take a mug from him.

"The kettle just boiled," he said to Rose.

"Thank you," she said, reaching up to pat his cheek. She headed upstairs, trailed, as usual, by Elvis.

"I'm getting the feeling that things didn't go so well," Mac said to me.

"Victoria did know that Ian was here," I said.

"Did she know he was alive the whole time?"

I shook my head. "She says she didn't."

"Do you believe her?"

"I do," I said. "He just came up to her when she was at the park with Rachel. He wanted some things that belonged to his mother." I took another sip of my coffee. "She said he wanted her to run away with him. Her and Rachel."

"Was she going to?" Mac asked.

"I can't say that surprises me," he said.

"Do you think she killed him?"

"No," Rose said.

I turned to look at her standing in the doorway. She was carrying a cup of tea. She smiled at Mr. P. and brought it to him.

"Thank you," he said. "I am a little parched."

I waited until he took a sip and made a little murmur of pleasure.

"Are you going to tell us how you managed to get Tim away from the house?" I asked.

"I admit, I'm curious," Rose added.

"Actually, I didn't do anything," Mr. P. said, looking at both of us over the top of his cup. "Unfortunately a seagull got into Mr. Harding's offices." He tried to look contrite but didn't quite pull it off.

Rose was smiling as if she knew something I didn't.

"A seagull?" I said. "It must have been very disruptive."

Mr. P. had another sip of his tea before he answered. "Yes, it was," he said. "Or so I heard. It was flying all round the office and it set off the alarm. The security person called Mr. Harding."

I eyed him with some suspicion. "No one killed an innocent seagull, did they?"

Mr. P. was horrified. "No. Merton came and collected it. I promise you the bird is fine. She's probably having a nice snack of sardines about now."

"Wait a minute," I said, holding up one hand. "How did Merton got involved?" The little old man seemed to be involved in a lot of my life at the moment.

Ian. Or maybe she figured out that her tenant Dan Cooper was really a presumed-dead con artist. Maybe she stopped by the cottage just by chance."

"That's a lot of maybes," Mr. P. said.

I blew out a breath. "Right now maybes are all we have."

Rose called the property management company and discovered Kendra was away until Saturday afternoon. The receptionist gave Kendra's cell number to Rose.

"I think we should wait and talk to Kendra in person," she said.

"I agree," Mr. P. said. He looked at me and I nodded.

"Me too," I said.

Two tour buses arrived about an hour apart and I didn't get to eat lunch until quarter to two. It was all hands on deck. We sold a lot of small things including all the teacup planters and all of the pillows Jess made, which often happened when a bus full of tourists stopped in. But I also sold two guitars and a wrought iron headboard, which Mac wrapped in two old blankets and he and the driver managed to stash in the luggage compartment of the bus despite the limited amount of space. Not the first time Mac had done that.

Rose left at two o'clock with Mr. P. in tow. "Don't make dinner plans," she said as she zipped up her windbreaker.

"Why?" I asked.

Mr. P. was attaching his magnetic clip-on sunglasses to his glasses. He looked up and smiled. "If we tell you it will ruin the surprise."

I needed some new running clothes. I tended to wear leggings and T-shirts until they were faded and worn and, like many other runners I knew, I spent my money on shoes.

I sat on the floor by the front door to put on my shoes, my favorite pair of Brooks. The shoes I had been wearing the day I had found Ian's body were still on the mat by the door waiting to be cleaned. Both shoes had streaks of red dirt across the toes, probably from when I'd climbed up the makeshift ladder holding Dexter the puppy.

Mr. P. had explained the soil was marine clay, soft with a high moisture content. The red color came from iron oxide.

My heart began to pound, thudding in my ears. Tim Harding had the same red streak on his running shoes. I'd noticed it the day we'd done the circuit of the park together.

Tim had been at the cottage.

Tim had been in the storm cellar.

It was too much of a coincidence otherwise. I thought about what Victoria had told Rose and me: Tim had gone running with one of his friends, the one who got him started. But the morning I'd done the circuit of the park with him he'd told me the friend who had gotten him into running had broken his ankle.

Had *Tim* killed Ian?

But he was right-handed. Right. Not left-handed. It didn't make sense. Was it possible Nick was wrong about the killer being left-handed? That didn't make sense, either. Nick didn't make those kinds of mistakes.

premeditated but he was still going to end up in jail and he would lose what mattered most to him."

"Victoria and Rachel," Rose said.

I nodded. "Yes."

"He gave Victoria an alibi because it gave him an alibi," she said slowly.

"I think so," I said. "When Mr. P. was showing Tim the aerial map of North Harbor that you have in the office Tim commented about Windspeare Point looking different from the ground. How did he know that? He lives on the opposite side of town."

Now came the part that was me going way out on a limb. "That dirt I noticed on Tim's shoes looked fresh," I said. "Like he'd gotten it on his shoes recently. Say that morning."

Rose looked puzzled. "And you think that's important?"

I nodded. I was jumpy, not sure what to do with my hands. "I know this is a huge leap but I think Tim is looking for the money."

"You mean the money Ian Stone took from his investors?"

"I think that's the reason Ian came back to North Harbor. Not for Victoria. Not for Rachel. For the money. Fiona said as much."

"But he asked Victoria to run away with him."

"I think he wanted something from her, something connected to the money, and making her think he still loved her was the easiest way to get whatever that was."

"But why didn't he just move the money to some

his investors and turned into gold bars or rare coins and we know all this because his shoes were dirty?"

She was right. The only evidence I had to support my reasoning was a streak of red dirt on Tim Harding's shoe. It wasn't exactly compelling. I exhaled loudly. "So what do we do?"

"We go try to find whatever it was Mr. Stone hid. Whatever it is, Tim Harding has been looking for it, and we keep our fingers crossed that it hasn't already been found. If we find whatever Tim has been searching for then we call Michelle and share what we suspect because then we'll have evidence."

I shifted restlessly from one foot to the other. "And what if we don't find anything?"

"Then we pull in Alfred and find enough evidence to make a case against Tim for killing Mr. Stone. I don't see any other options." She had that resolute look in her eye that I'd seen many times in the past.

I didn't see any other options, either. "All right," I reluctantly agreed.

Rose put on her gray windbreaker and I got my car keys. I knew there wouldn't be a lot of traffic so early on a Saturday morning. We climbed in the car, and I hoped this didn't turn out to be a bad idea.

"Take the next right," Rose said as we got close to Windspeare Point.

"Why?" I asked.

"Because I don't think we should park directly in front of the cottage. I don't know if Tim would recognize this vehicle but Ashley or Keenan certainly

"Something small and portable."

"So not gold bars."

I shook my head. "Ian was supposed to have stolen somewhere around a hundred million dollars. That would be a lot of gold bars. Maybe gold coins, though. Something like that would be a lot easier to move around."

"You think it's in the storm cellar," Rose said.

"I do," I said. "Think about it. Not a lot of people know those old cellars even exist. Ian came to town. Retrieved the coins or whatever he'd turned the money into and hid them in the storm cellar for safekeeping. Maybe he even suspected Tim was onto him and he didn't want to hide anything in the cottage."

We headed across the lawn.

"Why didn't he just leave everything in his original hiding place?"

"Because the original hiding place was Victoria."

Rose stopped walking. "So you're saying she lied to us."

"No," I said. "I think it's likely Ian turned the money into gold coins or uncut diamonds, probably in the weeks before the Ireland trip. Do you remember Victoria saying he asked her for some things that had belonged to his mother?"

"The puzzle box."

I nodded.

"You think he hid diamonds or gold coins worth close to a hundred million dollars in a wooden box and left it with his ex-wife? That was risky. She could have gotten rid of it."

I don't think he had any idea where it was, by the way. It's the only thing that makes sense."

Rose was silent for what felt like a very long time. "You're right," she said at last. "It *is* the one explanation that makes sense. And there isn't anything we can do about it right now."

I nodded in agreement.

We started walking again toward the backyard.

A tarp was spread over the entrance to the storm cellar, the edges held down by large rocks. It took the two of us to move them but after a few minutes of work I was able to peel back the edge of the plastic. The actual cellar opening was covered with long boards. Nothing was really fastened down very securely. I remembered Kendra telling Rose and me that at some point everything was going to be filled in. This might be the last chance I'd have to look around down there.

I used the flashlight on my phone to look down into the cellar. To my surprise the ladder was still down there, lying on the floor next to the far side wall.

"The ladder is down there," I said to Rose. "I'm going to jump down and take a look around. I can climb up the way I did before."

She gave my arm a squeeze. "Okay, sweet girl. Just be careful."

I swung my legs over the side of the opening, hung for a moment and then dropped to the bottom. I straightened up and looked around. I could see that Tim or someone had been down there looking for something. There were several holes dug in the clay floor, including in the far corner where I'd found

Chapter 20

"I'm all right," Rose said.

"Good," I said. She didn't look hurt, which eased my sense of panic just a little. I looked at Tim. "Please let her go."

"I can't do that," he said. "The moment I do she'll call the police."

Rose nodded. "He's right. I would do that."

I kept my eyes glued to Tim's face. I had to either talk him down or get the knife away from Rose's neck. "What do you want?" I asked.

He sighed. "What I want is for Ian Stone, brilliant financial adviser turned scumbag con artist, to have stayed fake dead."

"You killed him."

"Yes. Not deliberately. It was an accident." He gestured at the hole behind me. "He fell down there and hit his head."

I knew he was lying. Ian had been hit over the

us down in the storm cellar and leave us there to die. Maybe hitting us both over the head the way he had with Ian. Either way, I knew I'd gotten us into this and I had to get us out.

"It won't work," I said. "No one will believe both of us fell down there."

"Sure they will," he said. "You're here, aren't you? You uncovered the storm cellar, didn't you?"

Rose caught my eye and glanced down at Tim's arm. "This could come back to bite you if you're wrong," she said. I knew that look of determination in her gray eyes.

She was going to bite him. *Rose was going to bite him.* I couldn't let that happen.

"Bad idea," I said to Tim. My eyes flicked to Rose for a second so she knew I was really talking to her. That determined gleam didn't change. I couldn't stop her. I was just going to have to give everything I had to protect her. When Rose bit Tim I was going to get that knife.

"I think it's a very good idea," Tim said. He motioned toward the open hole in the ground behind me with the hand that held the knife. "Move."

I crossed my arms over my chest. "No," I said.

He brandished the knife. "I *will* cut her," he said.

What happened next seemed to occur in slow motion even though in reality it only took a second or two. Rose bit down hard on Tim's right arm. I lunged for the other one. And Casey came out of nowhere running at top speed. The dog hit Tim in the middle of his back, pushing him to the ground. Rose somehow managed to pull away at the last minute. She

responding officer could check on him. The dog stationed himself in front of Rose and I had no doubt he'd launch himself onto Tim again if he felt Rose was threatened in any way. Keenan eventually appeared, more than a little confused to find the police—and us—at the cottage once again. He took a very reluctant Casey home.

Michelle arrived and listened to the condensed version of what had happened without commenting, arms folded over her chest. The longer she didn't say anything the more worried I got.

"This wasn't Sarah's idea," Rose said. "It was mine."

"I'm not surprised," Michelle said. Her gaze never left my face. "You've done some stupid things, Sarah, but this is the stupidest."

"I'm pretty sure I've done some dumber stuff than this," I said, regretting the flippant words the moment they were out of my mouth.

Rose put a hand on my arm. "Don't," she said softly.

"Not funny," Michelle snapped. "You could have gotten Rose killed. You could have gotten yourself killed. I expect more from you." She took a shaky deep breath and let it out. "Go," she said. "You're free to leave. I don't want to talk to you." She walked away from us.

I just stood there. I didn't know what I could say to repair things. This time I couldn't hold back the tears. Rose put one arm around me. "Don't worry," she said. "We can fix this."

I wasn't so sure we could.

Chapter 21

Rose had already called Mac. She didn't say what she had told him and I didn't ask, but I suspected that she had downplayed what had happened. We drove back to the house to get cleaned up. It was just starting to rain and the bleak, gray sky matched my mood.

Rose laid a hand against my cheek for a moment. "Go take a shower," she said. "You'll feel better when you're cleaned up."

I stood under the hot water longer than I needed to. Michelle and I had had a falling-out when we were teenagers—due to my bad behavior—and we had rekindled our friendship in only the last couple of years. It made me sick to think that something stupid I'd done might have destroyed it again.

Elvis had followed me into the bathroom, somehow

"As I recall, you did." She studied my face for a long moment. "Do you consider me old and feeble?" she asked.

I stared at her. "What? No. You're neither of those things."

"Then stop acting as though that's what you think. Maybe it wasn't the finest moment for either one of us, but we're both sitting here, pretty much intact, while Tim Harding is in handcuffs. It seems to me things worked out pretty well."

I nodded. "It was Casey's finest moment. How did he know?"

Rose shook her head. "I have no idea. We just seem to have a connection."

I was fervently glad they did.

We collected Elvis and headed for the shop. Mac and Mr. P. were waiting when we stepped inside. Mr. P. took Rose's hands and studied her face. I could see the concern in his eyes.

"Are you all right?" he asked.

She smiled at him. "I'm fine, Alf," she said. "I promise."

He turned to look at me.

"She is," I said. "She's also very resourceful."

Rose and I exchanged a smile. "And maybe just a tiny bit foolhardy," she said.

"Are you all right, my dear?" Mr. P. asked me.

I nodded. "Aside from two skinned knees, I'm good, too."

"I could use a cup of tea," Rose said.

*   *   *

I kept hoping that Michelle would show up at some point but she didn't. Nick came by just before lunch and read Rose and me the riot act. When he was finished—which took a while—Rose wrapped him in a hug. "I love you," she said, kissing his cheek.

At the end of the day Liz arrived to collect Rose and Mr. P. along with Avery. They were picking up Greg, and all of them were going out to dinner. She was carrying a brown paper shopping bag, which she handed to Mac. "Dinner," she said. She turned to me. "I would yell at you over this whole escapade but I'm the one who put it in motion and according to Rose everything you did was to protect her. So I won't. Don't do this again."

"I won't," I said.

"I can't stay," she said. "We're taking dinner to the dog first." She turned in the doorway and blew me a kiss. "Try to stay out of trouble, toots."

Monday morning Fiona showed up at the shop. "Thank you for finding my . . . Ian's killer," she said. She explained that Victoria had disappeared with Rachel. The police were looking for her. Among other things she had kept the fact that Ian was alive a secret and she had lied when the police questioned her. If—when—they found her she'd face criminal charges.

According to Nick, Tim's lawyer was working on a plea deal for his client. He was going to spend a long time in jail. Once everything was settled the investors would get most of their money back. That much at least made for a happy ending.

Michelle arrived a couple of minutes before ten. Rose brought her up to my office. I got to my feet and cleared my throat. "I, um . . . Thank you for coming," I said.

She nodded. "You're welcome."

"You were—are right," I began. "What I did was the stupidest thing I've ever done because it put Rose at risk. And she . . . means the world to me." My voice seemed to be stuck in my throat. "Rose is one of the best people I know with a heart bigger than anyone else's I've ever known. I am so, so sorry for being so reckless. I'm sorry for putting her at risk and I'm sorrier than you can imagine that I damaged my friendship with you."

I was holding an envelope and I held it up so Michelle could see it. "She gave me this to give to you because she hoped it might repair things between us." I looked over at Rose, who smiled at me. "That's the kind of person she is. But I had nothing to do with what's inside." I handed the envelope to Rose. "You should give it to her," I said.

Rose caught my hand and gave it a squeeze. Then she handed the envelope to Michelle. "Open it, please," she said.

Michelle undid the flap and pulled out a photograph of a house. It was a craftsman cottage, painted gray-green with light gray on the double dormers and porch columns and sand brown trim. The grass out front was neatly trimmed.

Michelle looked up from the photo, a frown creasing her forehead. "What is this?" she asked.

Rose looked at me. "Tell her," she said.

"Okay," I said.

She left. My legs were trembling so hard I was afraid to try to sit down because I was pretty sure I'd fall.

Rose reached over and patted my arm. "See?" she said. "I told you. Things have a way of working out."

I gave her a hug. "Yes, they do," I said.

Acknowledgments

There are dozens of people who have worked very hard to create and promote this book and all the others in the Second Chance Cat Mysteries—from art and editorial to production, marketing, publicity, accounting, warehousing and more. None of the books would exist without their efforts. Thank you, everyone. Thanks as well to my editor, Jessica Wade, and my agent, Kim Lionetti, who work tirelessly—and cheerfully—on my behalf. And as always, thanks to Patrick and Lauren, who always have my back and my heart.

Love Elvis the cat?
Then meet Hercules and Owen!
Read on for an excerpt from
the first book by Sofie Kelly
in the Magical Cats Mysteries . . .

CURIOSITY THRILLED THE CAT

Available in paperback
from Berkley Prime Crime!

The body was smack in the middle of my freshly scrubbed kitchen floor. Fred the Funky Chicken, minus his head.

"Owen!" I said sharply.

Nothing.

"Owen, you little fur ball, I know you did this. Where are you?"

There was a muffled "meow" from the back door. I leaned around the cupboards. Owen was sprawled on his back in front of the screen door, a neon yellow feather sticking out of his mouth. He rolled over onto his side and looked at me with the same goofy expression I used to get from stoned students coming into the BU library.

I crouched down next to the gray-and-white tabby. "Owen, you killed Fred," I said. "That's the third chicken this week."

The cat sat up slowly and stretched. He padded over to me and put one paw on my knee. Tipping his near anything and Owen squirmed with joy. Hercules, on the other hand, was indifferent.

The stocky black-and-white cat climbed onto my lap, too. He put one white paw on my shoulder and swatted at my hair.

"Behind the ear?" I asked.

"Meow," the cat said.

I took that as a yes, and tucked the strands back behind my ear. I was used to long hair, but I'd cut mine several months ago. I was still adjusting to the change in style. At least I hadn't given in to the impulse to dye my dark brown hair blond.

"Maybe I'll ask Rebecca if she has any ideas for my hair," I said. "She's supposed to be back tonight." At the sound of Rebecca's name Owen lifted his head. He'd taken to Rebecca from the first moment he'd seen her, about two weeks after I'd brought the cats home.

Both Owen and Hercules had been feral kittens. I'd found them, or more truthfully they'd found me, about a month after I'd arrived in town. I had no idea how old they were. They were affectionate with me, but wouldn't allow anyone else to come near them, let alone touch them. That hadn't stopped Rebecca, my backyard neighbor, from trying. She'd been buying both cats little catnip toys for weeks now, but all she'd done was turn Owen into a chicken-decapitating catnip junkie. She was on vacation right now, but Owen had clearly managed to unearth a chicken from a secret stash somewhere.

I stroked the top of his head again. "Go back to

their mother. They were so small and so determined to come with me that in the end I'd brought them home.

There were whispers around town about Wisteria Hill and the feral cats. But that didn't mean there was anything unusual about my cats. Oh no, nothing unusual at all. It didn't matter that I'd heard rumors about strange lights and ghosts. No one had lived at the estate for quite a while, but Everett refused to sell it or do anything with the property. I'd heard that he'd grown up at Wisteria Hill. Maybe that was why he didn't want to change anything.

Speaking of not wanting change, Hercules was not eager to relinquish his prime spot on my lap. But after some gentle prodding, he shook himself and got off. Owen yawned a couple of times, stretched and took twice as long to move.

I got the broom and dustpan from the porch and swept up the remains of Fred the Funky Chicken. Owen and Hercules sat in front of the refrigerator and watched. Owen made a move toward the dustpan, like he was toying with the idea of grabbing the body and making a run for it.

I glared at him. "Don't even think about it."

He sat back down, making low, grumbling meows in his throat.

I flipped open the lid of the garbage can and held the pan over the top. "Fred was a good chicken," I said solemnly. "He was a funky chicken and we'll miss him."

"Meow," Owen yowled.

I dumped what was left of the catnip toy into the garbage. "Rest in peace, Fred," I said as the lid closed.

town for the last several months. And why I'd be here for the next year and a half. I was supervising the restoration—which was almost finished—as well as updating the collections, computerizing the card catalog and setting up free internet access for the library patrons. I was slowly learning the reading history of everyone in town. It made me feel like I knew the people a little, as well.

ABOUT THE AUTHOR

Sofie Ryan is a writer and mixed-media artist who loves to repurpose things in her life and in her art. She is the author of *Scaredy Cat, Totally Pawstruck,* and *Undercover Kitty* in the *New York Times* bestselling Second Chance Cat Mysteries. She also writes the *New York Times* bestselling Magical Cats Mysteries under the name Sofie Kelly.

VISIT SOFIE RYAN ONLINE

SofieRyan.com